Darren is a dhampir, and like all dhampirs, he hates vampires. He hates them even more since they captured him and are holding him prisoner, or at least, that's what he tries to convince himself.

Caley is a medical examiner for the conclave, and since the dhampirs arrived in town, he's been overworked. That hasn't stopped him from being fascinated by Darren, even though being interested in a vampire hunter is the worst thing that could happen to a vampire — especially when he's tasked with keeping an eye on the hunter.

Darren wants out of his cell. The conclave wants more information from him. By letting him stay with Caley, everyone gets what they want.

Until Caley and Darren fall in love.

Darren has been raised to hate vampires, but he can't anymore. His father still leads the dhampirs, though, and they're tearing through the city. Darren can help stop him, but is he ready to sacrifice himself and what he found with Caley to do that?

Despised Fangs
Copyright © 2021 Catherine Lievens
ISBN: 978-1-4874-3173-0
Cover art by Angela Waters

Published by eXtasy Books Inc or
Devine Destinies, an imprint of eXtasy Books Inc

Look for us online at:
www.eXtasybooks.com or www.devinedestinies.com

DESPISED FANGS
LIFE WITH FANGS 6

BY

CATHERINE LIEVENS

CHAPTER ONE

Darren stared at the door of his cell.

He was bored.

He didn't know how long he'd been locked up, but he supposed it didn't matter. It wasn't like he'd be let free anytime soon. He had a hard time getting used to it, though. He hated being locked up and having to look at the same four walls day after day, week after week.

But he was lucky. He didn't know what had happened to the other dhampirs he'd worked with before being captured, but he could imagine. They probably weren't in a nice cell the way he was. If they were lucky, their death had been swift.

The only reason Darren hadn't been killed was that he'd agreed to help the vampires. His father would kill him if he ever found out about this, so all in all, Darren didn't mind being stuck here that much. It was better than having to deal with his father, which was why he hadn't protested much the past few times Oren had visited him for information. He always made a point of bitching, but his heart wasn't in it.

If he was honest, the situation wasn't as bad as it could be. For one, he wasn't dead. The cell also wasn't what he'd imagined the vampires would stick him in if they ever caught him. He'd thought it would be small, dark, and damp. Instead, it was comfortable. The mattress was soft, as was the pillow. He had plenty of blankets, and he needed them, since the cell was always cold. But he even had a TV and a small table with a chair where he ate his meals.

And they were good. He wasn't starving like he'd

expected. He had no idea who cooked, since vampires only drank blood, but whoever did was a good cook.

Darren had no idea how long he was going to be stuck here, and while he wasn't looking forward to it, it was better than the alternative. He was grateful that the vampires hadn't killed him. It would have turned him into a vampire, and though he'd discovered that not all vampires were monsters like his father had always told him, he wasn't looking forward to an immortal life drinking blood and staying out of the sun.

He liked being tanned, thank you very much.

When he heard footsteps come closer, he sat up on his bed and stared at the cell door. It was too soon for his next meal, so it had to be something else. Did Oren need more information? Darren wouldn't be surprised. He knew what his father was planning, even though he hadn't told anyone about it. Dhampirs would continue arriving in town in waves, and they wouldn't leave, not alive. The problem was that killing them turned them into vampires, which was something no one wanted. Dhampirs were vampire hunters because of what they were, and vampires didn't want to create vampires who hated them and would have an easy time killing them once they were immortal.

A key slid into the lock, and the cell door creaked open. Darren peeked up, but it wasn't Oren. A guard stood there, peering in, and Darren grinned. He knew that some vampires, especially younger ones, were fascinated by him. He understood it. There weren't a lot of dhampirs around, and they were no doubt curious.

He raised his hand and wiggled his fingers. "You need me?" he asked.

The vampire straightened, and Darren was pretty sure he was blushing. He hadn't even realized it was possible. "There's someone here to see you."

"Oh? Who is it?"

"Falkner."

Darren grumbled, but he was secretly happy to see Falkner. "Do I really have to go?"

The guard looked nonplussed. "I suppose not, but I should let him know. Do you want to stay in your cell?"

This guard was no fun. Oren always snarked back, and he and Darren ended up bickering with each other. It gave Darren a distraction. "No." He got to his feet. "I'll come." If anything, it would distract him for a moment. He would be bored again soon enough.

Darren stretched, grinning when he saw the vampire was staring at him. He made a show out of it, even though he had no intention of doing anything more. He didn't know if the vampire was just fascinated with him or if there was something more there, but he wasn't about to have a relationship with anyone, let alone a vampire.

"Where to?" he asked as he stepped closer to the door.

"The interrogation room."

"You know, you guys really should have a room dedicated to this. Where do the other prisoners meet their families?"

"They don't."

Darren supposed that answered his question. "Why not?"

"Because they don't stay prisoners for long."

Because they died. He didn't have to say it for Darren to understand. "Is anyone planning on killing me?" He made sure to keep his voice light, even though he was tense. If something was going to happen to him, he wanted to know.

"Not as far as I know. Oren forbid anyone touching you in any way."

"I knew he liked me."

"I think he likes the information you can give him more."

Darren huffed. "Way to break my heart."

The vampire stepped aside so Darren could move into the hallway. He didn't bother handcuffing Darren, but then,

Darren couldn't go anywhere. There was no way for him to run, and even though he could attack the guard, it wouldn't be useful. He was just a human, and without weapons and help, he was useless against the vampire.

So Darren walked next to the guard, looking around and making the most out of the situation. He would be back in his cell soon enough, even though he wasn't looking forward to it.

The guard didn't come into the interrogation room with him. Instead, he opened the door and let Darren in before closing and locking it behind him.

Falkner was sitting at the table, and he smiled when he saw Darren. He got to his feet, maybe to hug Darren.

Darren was horrified at the thought. "What are you doing here?"

Falkner didn't look angry at Darren's harsh words. "I'm here to see you, of course."

"You shouldn't continue to come. It doesn't make sense, and I can't imagine your boyfriends are happy about it. Who came with you today?"

"Andrew. And you're right. He wasn't happy. I won't stop coming, though."

"Why not?" Darren knew he was pushing too hard. He might have told Falkner to stay away, but he was secretly happy and incredulous, and he didn't want their friendship to stop. He didn't understand why Falkner was doing this, but if Falkner didn't come to visit, he would be alone most of the time. He still was, but he looked forward to the weekly visits from Falkner. Sometimes he came even more often. It was a break from a boring routine, but it also made Darren feel like someone cared.

His father certainly wouldn't. He had to know what had happened to Darren, although maybe he didn't know that Darren was still alive. The other dhampirs wouldn't be, and that, he *would* be aware of. Darren didn't think his father would care even if he were dead, which was one of the reasons he was happy Falkner did.

Falkner didn't owe him anything. *Darren* owed *him,* since Falkner had almost killed him, but instead of being angry and demanding Darren's head on a silver platter, Falkner visited him and acted as if they were friends. It didn't make sense, but Darren had stopped trying to understand what was going on in Falkner's mind.

"Because we're friends," Falkner said simply.

"I'm pretty sure friends don't try to kill each other."

Falkner smiled. "You didn't try to kill me, not really."

"All right. Then, I tried to use you to get to your coven."

"You did, but your heart wasn't in it."

Darren was mildly offended. "What are you talking about? Of course my heart was in it."

Falkner arched a brow, but he didn't call out Darren's lie. "Why don't you sit down?"

Darren huffed, but he obeyed. He was glad Falkner wasn't going anywhere, even though he didn't understand why.

Caley washed his hands, glad to get the feeling of the latex gloves off his skin. They were a necessity in his work, but it didn't mean he had to like them.

He didn't.

He supposed that once he would have performed autopsies without them if he'd already been doing this job. The thought made him shiver, though. He might be a vampire, but that didn't mean he wanted to stick his hands into a dead body and get blood all over himself.

If he got hungry, he knew where the cafeteria was.

He turned off the water, dried his hands, and took a deep breath.

At least this vampire hadn't been killed by dhampirs. They were getting crueler in their killings, and Caley wasn't looking forward to performing autopsies on their victims. He never was, but they were increasingly aggressive, and something was going to break sooner rather than later.

Caley's gaze drifted toward another body. He'd performed the autopsy on her yesterday, and she *had* been killed by dhampirs. He didn't have proof of it, but he believed he was right. She'd been drugged and beheaded, and that was how dhampirs worked these days. They drugged vampires so they'd be sluggish and unable to escape, and once they were sure the vampire wouldn't attack, they beheaded them. It was a straightforward autopsy, but Caley didn't like it.

He pushed away from the sink and headed out. He needed some time away from the autopsy room.

He should have known it wouldn't be that easy. He wasn't surprised to find Oren waiting for him outside. Oren, unlike a lot of people Caley worked with, didn't mind coming into the room—or rather, he made a point of coming in. He wasn't responsible for the people on the tables, but he was the one who had to investigate their deaths, at least in part. There were other team leaders, but none of them were quite as focused as Oren. He was always there, asking if Caley had an update, if he knew what had happened to the bodies they brought in.

"I thought it was going to take a while longer," Oren said.

Caley sighed. "It's becoming routine at this point. I know what to look for, which is why it doesn't take me as long as usual. I autopsied her yesterday, but I got a few more results today."

Oren's expression was stiff. "Dhampirs?"

Caley nodded. "I'm pretty sure, yes. It's the same MO, at the very least. You know I can't be a hundred percent sure it was them, but if I had to guess, I would say the dhampirs are still killing vampires in town." His frown deepened. "I thought they'd been eliminated." Or rather, he'd hoped they had been.

Oren sighed and rubbed his face. He looked tired, which made sense, considering what was happening. "There are a lot of different dhampir groups, unfortunately. I don't know why, but they're all flocking to town, which results in more vampires getting killed."

Caley grimaced. "Which means I'm going to have a lot more clients before this is over."

"I'm doing everything I can, but unfortunately, it's not a lot. The conclave recalled several teams, so we have more manpower now, but it's still not enough. The city is big, and there aren't enough of us to patrol it. We've been asking the covens to make sure their vampires stay home as much as possible, but there's always someone who doesn't obey. And of course, some vampires don't belong to a coven and have to leave their homes for one reason or another."

"What then? Someone has to do something. We can't allow the dhampirs to continue killing vampires. There won't be any of us left if they do." It was an exaggeration, but with the number of bodies Caley had taken care of lately, it wasn't even that much of a stretch. There'd been an uptick of work for him since the dhampirs had arrived in town, and he couldn't wait for them to leave. He doubted that would happen anytime soon, though. Dhampirs killed vampires, and there were plenty of those in town.

"I'm going to have to talk to Darren again," Oren said.

That got Caley's attention. "You're not happy about it."

"I'd rather not have to deal with him. It's not easy."

"What did you expect? For him to tell you everything you want to know just because you asked? He's not just a dhampir. He's also a prisoner, and he's not going to forget that."

Oren snorted and pushed away from the wall he'd been leaning against. "He might be a prisoner, but he's treated well. I don't know what he has to whine about."

Caley pressed his lips together. He didn't want to smile and make Oren think he didn't take him seriously. "He might have a TV and blankets, but it doesn't mean he's not a prisoner. He can't leave his cell. He's not free to go wherever he wants to go."

"To kill vampires?"

Caley chuckled. "I suppose. I don't know him, so I can't answer. Are you going to talk to him now?"

"I might as well."

"Can I come with you?"

Oren frowned. "Why would you want to come with me?"

"Because I find him interesting. I won't go into the room with you, if that's what you're worried about. I can watch from outside."

"You can if you want, but I don't understand why you would."

"I suppose I'm curious. He's a dhampir, and until recently, they were extremely rare."

"I think they still are. The fact that they gathered into groups to kill us is worrying, and it's making their numbers feel bigger. From what I was able to find out, the dhampirs recruit all over the world."

"So there are dhampirs from all over the world in the city? Are you sure you don't know why they're gathering here?"

"No idea. Maybe they realized the conclave has a base here, and they want to get rid of it."

"The conclave has a lot of bases, though." It didn't make sense, but Caley couldn't think of another explanation.

He and Oren walked down the hallway. Caley had been planning on going to the cafeteria to grab some blood, but this was better. He wasn't in a rush anyway. All his patients were dead, and even though he wanted to give them justice, he wouldn't be the one doing that. Oren and the other team leaders and members would, and Caley was more than happy to stay back. It wasn't his job, but he did everything he could to help.

"Whatever's going on, they have to have a plan," Oren murmured.

"And it can't be good for vampires."

"I doubt it will be. If I had to guess, they're planning on eradicating the vampires from the city. I suppose that once they manage, they'll move on to the next one, then the next one. Their goal is to have a world without vampires, and it scares me that they already have such a good head start."

It scared Caley, too. Vampires were usually careful and wary of people they didn't know. They had to learn to be if they didn't want to be killed. The dhampirs weren't the only ones hunting vampires, unfortunately. It was something vampires learned soon after they were made.

Most of the vampires who had ended up on Caley's tables recently were young, though. It would make sense that they didn't know to be careful the way older vampires did. Still, even though there were a lot of vampires in the city, their numbers were dwindling. The conclave had had to call more teams from out of state, and while that helped, dhampirs were still killing their way through the city.

"You think Darren will be able to tell you anything?" Caley asked as they reached the interrogation room.

"I don't know, but I hope so. I need him to help us."

"What if he doesn't want to?"

Oren's expression was grim. "Then, he won't be useful to us anymore. We won't have a reason to keep him the way we have been."

"Will you kill him?"

"We'll make sure he dies, yes. The only reason he hasn't

yet, like the other dhampirs we captured with him, is that he's been useful. If he stops helping, though . . ."

Oren didn't have to repeat himself for Caley to understand.

Darren and Falkner were talking when the door opened. Darren expected it to be the guard who had let him out of his cell earlier, but it wasn't.

It was Oren, and the vampire was scowling.

Darren wasn't surprised. Oren was always scowling, especially when Darren was involved.

"I should have known I'd find both of you here," Oren mumbled.

Darren beamed at him. "You decided to come and have a chat with us. I knew you liked me."

"I hate you. But yes, I'm here to have a chat."

His tone told Darren that something had happened, and he could too easily imagine what. His stomach felt like it had turned to lead, and he had to force himself to keep the smile on his face. "Oh?"

Oren looked at Falkner. "You should leave."

Falkner was frowning, and he looked worried. Darren knew he had reason to be.

The dhampirs were still in town. Darren didn't know why his father had been focused on this city, but he suspected that part of it was that he wanted Darren back. Not because he loved him or because he cared about him, but because he couldn't allow vampires to use his son against him. If he ever got his hands on Darren, he would probably kill him because he was weak or something like that, which was one of the reasons Darren was more than happy to stay right where he was.

"I'll be back soon," Falkner told Darren.

"Well, you know where I'll be. Feel free to come anytime."

"This isn't a house visit," Oren snarked. "You can't get

visitors anytime you want."

Darren didn't point out that it was exactly how it worked, at least until now. From Oren's tone, though, he would make sure it changed if Darren said the wrong thing.

They both watched Falkner leave. As soon as the door was closed behind him, Darren allowed the smile to drop from his lips. "What happened?"

Oren sat in the empty chair on the other side of the table. "We had another death."

"How?"

"Drugged and beheaded."

Darren nodded. "The dhampirs."

"That's what we suspect. Why are so many of them in the city? It doesn't matter how many we find and capture. There are always more clusters. They seem to pop up from out of nowhere, and we don't understand why."

Darren bit his lower lip. He wanted to tell Oren about his father, but Oren wasn't his friend. Whatever was said in this room, Oren would report it to his superiors, who would then decide what to do with Darren. No matter how much Darren wanted to hope that the information he'd already given the vampires meant he was safe, he knew that wasn't the case.

He was a prisoner, after all.

He had to be careful and remember that Oren wasn't his friend. He didn't have friends, not even Falkner. He doubted Falkner would go running to Oren if Darren ever let something escape that he shouldn't, but he couldn't be sure.

"Well, you know that there are a lot of dhampirs in the world, right?" he asked as he leaned against his chair.

"I'm aware of that. What I want to know is why they're all arriving in town."

"How would I know? I've been stuck here for weeks. I don't know what's going on with the dhampirs anymore, and I doubt they would tell me even if you let me go."

Oren crossed his arms over his chest. "We're not letting you go."

"I didn't expect you to. I'm not sure what more you want from me, though. I've already told you everything I know."

"We both know that's not the truth."

Oren wasn't an idiot, so Darren wasn't surprised he was aware of that. "Oh? Do you want to hear about my first crush? His name was Mark, and—"

Oren slammed his hand on the table. "Don't play with me, Darren. We both know I can make your life hell if I want to."

"Why haven't you, then?" That was something Darren had been wondering since he'd been captured. He understood why Oren hadn't killed him like he had the other dhampirs, but he also didn't have to make Darren's life easier. Even though Darren only saw him when he wanted to talk to him like this, he knew that Oren was the one behind the TV in his cell and extra blankets.

He didn't understand. Oren hated him. It made sense, since he was a dhampir, and he killed vampires for work and pleasure. Why was Oren treating him so well, then? It couldn't just be Falkner's influence, surely.

Oren pinched the bridge of his nose.

Darren always seemed to push him to the edge, and he was waiting for Oren to break. He wasn't sure it would ever happen, but he was having fun trying.

"Because so far, you've been useful. Even though you haven't told me everything you know, you've told me the information I needed. You have to do it in this case, too. Why are the dhampirs here, and what do they want?"

Darren tapped his fingertips on his thigh as he considered the question. He couldn't tell Oren about his father. He didn't trust Oren, and who knew what Oren would do with that information. He had to give him something, though.

He really liked his blankets, and he didn't want them to be

taken away.

"They don't want anything you can give them," he finally said. "They want all vampires to die, which is what they're working toward. It's how they do it."

"I've never heard about so many dhampirs answering to one person." Oren stared at Darren. "Because that's how it's working, isn't it? There's no way for so many small groups to learn to work together without killing each other. There's someone in charge, and whoever it is, targeted the city. Why? Who are we talking about?"

"Why do you think I would know that?"

"Because you're a dhampir."

"And you think all dhampirs know the guy in charge? I don't." Even though the guy in charge was his father, he didn't truly know the man. He didn't want to get to know him, either.

"Tell me what you do know, then."

"Not a lot. It's what dhampirs do. They choose a city, put as many dhampirs in it as possible, and kill as many vampires as they can. Once they're done, they move on to the next city. You're just unlucky to be the chosen one this time."

"What can we do?"

Darren opened his hands. "I have no idea. You're the guy in charge, not me. I told you what I could."

"There's more."

There was, but Darren wasn't about to say it. "Not really."

"You were in charge of your dhampir group. You have to know more."

"I might have been in charge, but anyone else could have easily been. I never had any real power. I got my orders from someone, and that's all I knew. You already caught that guy, by the way, so there's no one else I can give you."

Oren stared at Darren. "You're lying again."

"What are you going to do about it?"

Oren growled. Clearly he was losing his patience, which was something Darren always thrived on. "You think this is a game? Vampires are *dying*."

"And I'm a vampire hunter. Don't you think I'm happy about that fact?"

"Is that why you're not telling me anything else? Because you want all vampires to die?"

Darren hesitated. He didn't want all vampires to die, not now that he'd realize not all of them deserved to die. Falkner was a good person, and under all the snark, so was Oren. "I just don't have anything else to tell you right now," he said instead of saying yes. For whatever reason, he didn't want to lie. He didn't want Oren to think badly of him.

He probably already did, and that didn't sit well with Darren, even though he didn't fully understand why.

But whatever Oren thought about Darren, Darren couldn't give him what he wanted. He couldn't tell him about his father or the reason the dhampirs were in town.

Because *he* was that reason.

Oren was frustrated. Caley could read the signs, and he was pretty sure Darren could, too. He was obviously poking at Oren and trying to make him lose his cool, which would be amusing if the situation weren't so dire.

"Why do you think he's doing this?" Falkner asked.

Caley hadn't been surprised to see Falkner sneak into the room to watch the interrogation. Caley didn't know why Darren was so important to Falkner, but it was obvious the man was. "Oren, or Darren?"

Falkner grinned. "I guess both of them, although I'm most interested in Darren. Why doesn't he want to help?"

"Why should he? As far as he's concerned, we're his enemies."

"But we've been treating him well. I think he knows that no other prisoner is allowed a TV in his cell and visitors every week."

"I have no doubt he does, but that doesn't make him less of a prisoner. He can't leave his cell, except to see you or to talk to Oren. I'm not one to want to go out and have fun, but sometimes, staying home or here becomes a lot. It's frustrating, and I need an outlet every so often. Darren doesn't have that. He can't leave the building, and even inside it, the only two rooms he ever sees are his cell and the interrogation room. It's been weeks, and it has to be taxing. There's also the fact that he probably thinks we're going to kill him once we have everything we want from him."

Falkner nodded as he stared at Darren. "I suppose you're right. He doesn't understand why the conclave is treating him like this."

"He doesn't understand because it doesn't make sense. He's using what he knows as leverage. If he doesn't have anything else to give us, he could be in trouble. He's in a kind of limbo, I suppose. He's not a vampire or entirely a prisoner. He's a traitor if he tells Oren more than he already has, although, in a way, he already is. It can't be easy."

Falkner turned his attention to Caley again. "I'm surprised that's what you think of him."

"What do you mean?"

"You sound sympathetic. Not a lot of people would be. No one understands why I'm so set on sticking with Darren and being his friend, not even my boyfriends. They think it's a kind of kinship because I'm a dhampir, but it's not just that. Darren needs a friend, and he didn't hurt me when he could have."

"He tried to use you, though."

"Isn't that what everyone does? We all try to use the people we know. Oren is trying to use Darren right now. Darren is trying to use Oren. It's just how human beings are."

What Falkner was saying made sense, and it gave Caley a better understanding of why Falkner was Darren's friend.

"You already told me a lot," Oren said in the interrogation room. "Why can't you tell me this, too?"

Darren looked annoyed, which was a pity. He was a gorgeous man, although that wasn't why Caley found him so fascinating.

All right, maybe it wasn't *only* because of that.

Like Caley's, Darren's hair was blond, but where Caley's hair was curly, Darren's was straight, and it had grown too long. His dark eyes were hard as he looked at Oren, but there was something lurking in them, something Caley wanted to identify.

But more importantly, Darren was a dhampir. So was Falkner, but Falkner had been a vampire for a long time. Darren, on the other hand, was still human, and it fascinated Caley. He wanted to find out more about the mechanism that created dhampirs. He wanted to find out how they became vampires if they died violently, but not if they died of old age or illness. He was a scientist at heart, and Darren played into that, even though he didn't even know Caley.

"I don't know anything else," Darren said. Everyone listening knew it was a lie.

This wasn't working. Oren was getting frustrated, which meant he was going to start yelling sooner or later. Darren was going to close himself off even more, and it wasn't going to help anyone.

Caley reached out and knocked on the glass that separated the room he and Falkner were in from the interrogation room. Oren's head snapped toward them, and he glared, but he still got up from his chair and headed toward the door.

"Leaving so soon?" Darren asked. He sounded like he didn't have a care in the world, but Caley thought he could detect a bit of anxiousness in his voice.

"Stay here and shut your mouth. I'll be right back," Oren snapped.

He slammed the door behind himself, and both Caley and Falkner winced.

"What do you want?" Oren said when he joined them.

"I was the one who knocked," Caley said. "What you're doing isn't working. I'd like to talk to him."

Oren's eyebrows shot up. "You want to talk to him?"

"It can't be worse than what you're doing right now."

"I got information from him in the past."

"You're right. You did, but it's not working now, and getting angry and yelling at him isn't going to change that."

"I can try," Oren said mulishly.

Caley sighed. "Of course you can. You're the boss, and you're the one making the decisions. You can go back in there and continue yelling at Darren until he tells you something, but I think we both know it's not going to happen. Don't you see? He's having fun poking at you and making you angry. You're playing his game."

Oren looked like he wanted to protest, but didn't. "You are *not* talking to him," he said.

"Why not? What you're doing isn't working, and a change might help."

"I'm not risking it. I'm not risking *you*."

Caley was touched. He and Oren had been friends for a long time, long enough for Caley to know everything and everyone Oren had lost. He knew Oren cared about him, but he hadn't realized he cared so much that he was ready to give up obtaining information just to keep Caley safe.

"He wouldn't hurt Caley," Falkner said. "I know what you think, but Darren isn't a bad person."

"He's a dhampir."

Falkner crossed his arms over his chest and arched a brow.

"So am I."

Oren looked embarrassed, but he didn't back down. "You're a vampire. What you were before doesn't matter. You're one of us, but he isn't. He's a vampire hunter, and he's dangerous. I don't care if he got you to believe he's harmless. He's not."

"I know he's not. He's trained, but what can he do right now? Caley is a vampire. So am I. Either one of us could talk to him and try to convince him to give us what he knows. It could save lives."

Oren hesitated, but Caley already knew from his expression they wouldn't win. "It could," he agreed. "It could also mean losing you or Caley, and I won't risk it. I know you're trying to do the right thing, but it's not going in there and talking to Darren. You should go home, Falkner."

"I wasn't done talking to Darren."

"You are for today, and the next time you come, make sure not to ask him about the dhampirs. He wouldn't take it well, and you might get hurt."

"He wouldn't hurt me." Falkner sounded convinced of that, and Caley thought he was right.

He understood why Oren was so wary and why he didn't want to risk it. He was a protector, and that included protecting Caley and Falkner. He was making a choice between them and the other vampires they could save by getting the information Darren had.

Caley was touched, but he wasn't sure it was the right thing to do. Even if it wasn't, though, there would be no talking Oren out of it. He'd made his decision, and he would stick by it.

He always did—well, almost always. The only one who had managed to get Oren to change his mind was Aubrey, Oren's boyfriend, and Caley was nowhere near as skilled as him.

CHAPTER TWO

When the cell door opened, Darren already knew who would be coming in. He sat up on his bed and grinned, especially since Oren looked annoyed. Darren knew Oren didn't like coming here, and it was one more opportunity for him to tease Oren. He couldn't wait. He needed all the fun he could get in this boring life of his.

Oren's expression told Darren that something had happened, though, and the smile slipped from his face. "What?" he asked.

Oren closed the cell door behind himself. He hovered there, staring at Darren until Darren wanted to squirm.

"What happened?" Darren asked again.

"The dhampirs killed a vampire couple," he said.

Darren blinked. "Well, I'm sorry, but it's kind of their job."

"This couple had recently adopted a human child. They were raising her as their own. She's dead, too."

Now Darren understood why Oren was horrified. It wasn't only because the child had been human, either. The dhampirs had killed a *child*, and that would be enough for anyone to be horrified. Darren swallowed. "Did they do it on purpose?"

Oren nodded curtly. "They did. We have witnesses. The child tried to run, and the dhampirs went after her. We don't know for sure yet, but it looks like she'd been drugged, too. They slit her throat. She was only seven."

Darren closed his eyes and tried to swallow again, but his mouth was dry. "I'm sorry."

"Why did they kill a human? I thought dhampirs tried to

protect humans from vampires."

Darren couldn't look Oren in the face as he answered. "They don't care about protecting humans. They only care about killing vampires. They probably thought the girl was tainted since she'd been adopted by two of them."

Oren raked a hand through his hair. "That doesn't even make sense."

"I never said it did. A lot of dhampirs are angry. They wish they were human, and they hate everyone who is, right along with vampires. The girl being tainted could have been an excuse, or they might just have wanted to kill her. Some dhampirs truly believe vampires and humans should be separated, but most don't care and kill just because they feel like it."

"What about you? Do you think she was tainted?"

Darren snorted. "Then I would be, too, wouldn't I?" Because he'd spent the past few weeks with vampires, and only vampires. If their presence tainted anyone, it was him.

He didn't believe it, though. He wasn't sure he'd ever truly believed it.

He'd been angry, and sometimes, he still was. His mother had abandoned him, and he'd never met her. His father had said she was probably living her best life out there, not even thinking about Darren, and that was one of the reasons Darren had started hunting vampires. Now that he'd had some time away from his father, he understood how his father had needled him and pushed him into becoming a hunter without ever telling him why he'd had a child with a vampire when he hated them so much.

It wasn't just his father's fault, though. Darren had his responsibilities, and he had to face them.

"We need your help," Oren said. "I know you said you were never in charge, and you've been here for several weeks, but you have to know something more about this. We have to stop them. They're not just killing vampires anymore. They're killing humans, *children*, and I can't allow that to continue. I could deal with it when they were killing vampires, but this is too much. You have to see that."

Darren did. He wanted to tell Oren everything, but he couldn't mention his father for his own protection. He could too easily imagine what would happen if he told Oren that his father was in charge of the vampire hunters. He was the one giving orders, and even though he probably hadn't ordered that child to be killed, he wouldn't have batted an eyelash at the knowledge. For him, humans were collateral damage. As long as the dhampirs killed as many vampires as possible, he didn't care who died. If the dhampirs did and turned, well, they'd end up on his killing list, and that was that.

Darren would, too, if he turned. He might have realized that not all vampires were evil bloodsuckers, but that didn't mean he wanted to be one. He'd been taught to hate vampires since he was old enough to walk. He'd rather die than become one.

But some dhampirs took advantage of the way Darren's father led them. They killed anyone they wanted, and if they were asked what had happened, they said they were just aiming for vampires or that they thought the human they'd killed had been tainted. It was enough for everyone to look the other way, and Darren had done the same thing.

He didn't think he could anymore.

He rubbed his face with both his hands. "I don't know what I can tell you."

"Anything would be useful at this point."

Darren looked at Oren. "What's going to happen to me if I tell you everything I know? Are you going to kill me like you killed the other dhampirs?"

Oren hesitated. "Of course not."

"We both know that's a lie. If I'm not useful to you, you

don't have a reason to keep me here. I'll only talk if we make a bargain."

Oren's expression closed off. "You want to bargain on the back of a little girl's death?"

It made Darren feel like shit, but he'd always been self-preserving. Anyone would be. He wanted to live, and he wanted to be free. He wasn't sure what being free meant at this moment, because he knew that if he ever left this building, he would probably die, but he'd had enough of his cell. "I'm sorry she's dead, and you're right. She shouldn't have been killed. If you know anything about the dhampirs who killed her, I can try telling you where you can find them. I can't make any promises, though. And I'm not trying to bargain on the back of her death. I'm just trying to protect myself. I'm sure you understand that."

Owen crossed his arms over his chest. He was still glaring, but Darren thought he'd won. It felt like a bitter victory, though.

It could have been him. He could have been the one to kill that little girl, and he hated himself for that. He'd grown up a vampire hunter. It was all he'd ever known, which was one of the reasons his father was no doubt disappointed at what Darren had managed to do when he'd been in charge of his team. His father had hoped Darren would eventually take his place as the vampire hunters' head, but Darren had never wanted that.

Now, he wasn't even sure he wanted to be a hunter.

"I want to leave this cell," he said slowly.

Oren's first reaction was to shake his head. "I can't allow that to happen. You're a prisoner."

"Then I'm sorry, but I don't have anything to tell you."

Oren looked like he was about to punch the wall. "How can you say that? You could save dozens of lives."

"I don't think I could. Whatever I know won't be enough

for you to catch all the dhampirs in town."

"But it would be something. It would be better than what we have now."

"It would be, yes. It would help catch at least a few dhampirs. I can't tell you anything until you make a few promises, though."

"And that includes letting you out of your cell."

Darren nodded. "I'm not asking for you to let me go entirely. I understand you can't do that, and I'm kind of resigned to the fact that I have to stick around. I'll still be a prisoner. I just want to leave this room. I'm getting cabin fever, and I need out."

Darren thought he saw a flash of understanding in Oren's gaze, but he had to be wrong. Oren wasn't understanding. When it came to Darren, he was hard and uncompromising.

"I'll have to talk to my superiors, and even if they agree, you won't be able to roam on your own. You'll have a guard," Oren said.

"Well, I'm not going anywhere. You have all the time you need to talk to them and try to convince them to let me out of the cell." Darren paused. "Of course, the sooner you do it, the sooner you'll get the information you want. That probably means fewer people will die, but the ball is in your court. And I refuse to be stuck with an enforcer. Find another way."

Oren's eyes narrowed. "I hate you."

That made Darren smile. "I know. I share that feeling."

Oren arched a brow. "You hate yourself?"

"I meant that I hate you." But he wasn't entirely wrong. Most days, Darren hated himself and what his life had become. It didn't have anything to do with being a prisoner, though.

Caley took a sip of blood and closed his eyes. He was

exhausted, and he wasn't even done working. He was used to long hours, but things were different now with dhampirs in town. He was working more than ever, and it was becoming harder and harder. Even now, he could see the image of that little girl being brought in, and he had to open his eyes for it to vanish.

He'd been a medical examiner for fifty years. If someone asked him why he'd chosen that profession, he wouldn't be able to answer. He could say that he wanted to give people who died peace and to help find their killer. It wouldn't be a lie. He did want to help as much as he could, and even though he was trained, he was done being an enforcer. He wasn't a fighter, no matter how good at it he was.

This was something he could do, though. He could examine bodies, find out why and how they'd died, and give that information to the investigators who would catch the killer.

It was getting harder, though. There were more bodies, and now, there was a child.

Caley wished he could say he'd thought the dhampirs wouldn't lower themselves to killing a child, but it would be a lie. He wasn't entirely surprised that they'd killed a child, not even a human child. It was horrifying, though. He wished he could find them, hurt them as much as they'd hurt the girl. Caley had been keeping her for last because he wasn't sure he could face it, but he was going to have to. First, though, there would be the mother.

He rubbed his forehead. Maybe it was time to ask the conclave for help. There hadn't been enough bodies for that until recently, but now, he couldn't keep up. If things continued going the way they were, he was going to need more staff.

The cafeteria door slammed, and Caley looked up to see Oren stomp his way inside. He looked around, and Caley knew Oren was looking for him. He raised a hand and waved, and Oren moved toward him. Several people had to jump out of the way, but Oren didn't seem to realize or care. He continued walking toward Caley, ignoring everything else.

Caley found it amusing. Aubrey had softened Oren somewhat, and he knew Oren was frustrated by that. He thought people wouldn't take him seriously if they knew how gentle and soft he was with his boyfriend, but Caley thought no one would care. Why would they? It was normal for Oren to be soft with his boyfriend. It was even normal for him to have a private life, a life away from the pain and death they had to deal with daily. Oren always wanted to appear strong, but as far as Caley was concerned, being able to leave the job at the door and focus on being loving and happy was a sign of being strong.

Oren finally reached him. He pulled out the chair on the other side of the table and flopped into it. Caley arched a brow, not used to seeing Oren this way. "What happened?" he asked.

"I tried talking to Darren."

"I see. It didn't go well?"

Oren threw his hands in the air. "When does it ever go well? I thought that telling him about the girl would help, but it didn't make any difference."

Caley found that hard to believe. "Do you want to talk about it?"

Oren rubbed his face, shook his head, then nodded. Caley chuckled, but he didn't say anything. He just waited. He knew his friend needed some time to gather his thoughts and put them into order, and he was more than happy to give him that time.

"I went to him. I told him what the dhampirs did, how they killed that little girl, even though she was human."

"What did he have to say about it?"

"He was sorry. I could see he was horrified, and I thought it meant he was finally going to help more."

"But he didn't." Caley didn't have to ask to know that.

"He has conditions."

Caley wasn't surprised, and he knew that if Oren took the time to think about it, he wouldn't be, either. "What kind of conditions?"

"He wants to be let out of the cell."

"He wants to be freed?"

"Not freed, no. He understands that we can't let him go. He just wants out of the cell. He offered to stay around the building, but I don't think I can trust him."

"You need to find him a babysitter."

"That's what I wanted to do, but he refuses to be stuck with an enforcer. Those are his words, by the way. Not mine."

"So he doesn't want to have to stay with an enforcer, but he also doesn't want to be stuck in his cell."

"That's pretty much it."

"Find someone else, then. It doesn't have to be an enforcer, as long as whoever you stick with him knows what they're doing. They have to know him, what he's capable of, and to be able to defend themselves if something happens."

"Where am I supposed to find such a person? All the people I know who are trained and capable are enforcers. Darren won't want to stay with any of them."

"What about Aubrey?"

"No." It was final.

Caley knew better than to push. He'd already known that would be the answer, but he still had to try. "Who then?"

Oren stared at him.

Caley narrowed his eyes, knowing he wouldn't like whatever was about to happen. "What?"

"You could do it," Oren said.

Caley arched a brow. "You didn't even want me to talk to him the other day. You said it was too dangerous and that you didn't want to risk me. What changed?"

"A little girl died. That's what changed. We have to do something, and we have to do it now before the dhampirs get even worse. They didn't stop killing a seven-year-old human. Do you really think they'll stop for *anything*?"

They wouldn't. Caley knew it, as did everyone else. They had to find a way to stop the dhampirs. "I'm sure there are people better suited to this than me."

"Not really. You were an enforcer before. You know what you're doing, how to defend yourself if Darren attacks you. You also know who he is and what he did. You're aware of how important he is to us, and how sneaky he can be. You're the best person to do it."

"It could be dangerous."

Oren grimaced. "It could be. It probably is. I don't think there's an alternative, though. We need to do something before someone else gets hurt, Caley. I hate asking this of you. I wish I didn't have to, but I don't see another way out of the situation. No matter how much I don't want any of this to happen, you're the best person to do this."

Caley swallowed. Oren was right. Besides, he'd been curious about Darren. This would be his chance to talk to the man and find out more about him.

He sighed. "I still think it's a terrible idea."

"I agree. It's the only idea we have, though. If you don't agree to it, I'll have to tell Darren no, and he won't talk."

"Are we even sure he has any kind of information about the dhampirs and what's happening? He's been here for weeks. He could be lying."

"It's a risk we're going to have to take, unfortunately. I wouldn't be surprised if he *was* lying, but the only way to find out is to give him what he wants. I'm not happy about it, but I don't think there's a way out of it."

Unfortunately, Caley agreed.

Darren was surprised when he next heard the sound of the key sliding into the door of his cell not even an hour after Oren had left. He'd expected Oren to ignore him for at least a few days, although he understood why he wouldn't. There was a sense of urgency now that the dhampirs had killed a human child. Even Darren felt it.

It made him feel guilty. He should be helping, but instead, he was thinking only about himself. He couldn't stop, though. This was his only chance to get a bit of freedom, and he was going to take it.

The door swung open, and Oren stepped in. He didn't look any different from how he had before, but there was a glint in his eyes, and Darren was instantly wary. "Miss me already?" he asked.

Oren didn't even answer. He closed the door behind himself and locked it again, then turned around and leaned against it, crossing his arms over his chest. It made the muscles in his arms bulge, and Darren allowed his gaze to linger on them.

It had been a while since he'd last seen a hot guy, and even longer since he'd had a night of fun with one. He couldn't deny Oren was hot, although he wasn't his type. Too big and bulky.

"What's going on?" Darren asked after Oren didn't answer. Usually, he was at the very least dismissive. Right now, though, he was only staring, and it was giving Darren the creeps.

"Will you give us the information we need?" Oren asked.

"If you give me what I want. If you want any kind of information from me, you'll let me out of this cell."

"All right."

Darren blinked. He had to have heard that wrong. "All right?"

"That's what I said. There are conditions, though."

Darren straightened. Of course there were. "What kind of conditions?"

"I'll allow you to stay with a friend of mine. That means you'll be able to leave the building, but you'll have to stay with him. The only two places you'll be able to go are this building and his apartment."

Darren narrowed his eyes. "I told you I didn't want to be babysat by an enforcer."

"Caley isn't an enforcer."

It sounded too good to be true, which was why Darren knew there was something more to it. "What aren't you telling me? Who is this Caley guy? Why do you seem so eager to dump me on him? Has he done something to you?"

Oren laughed.

Darren found himself blinking at him. He didn't think he'd ever heard Oren laugh. He was pretty sure there wasn't a lot of humor in the laughter, but it was still surprising.

"Caley hasn't done anything to me. He's a good friend. He's the only one who makes sense. Everyone else is an enforcer, but since you don't want to stay with one, it will have to be him."

"There's a catch. There has to be."

"No catches. I promise."

"And you expect me to believe you?"

Oren shook his head. "Of course not. You're going to have to, if you want to get out of here, though. It's him or nothing."

"You're ready to sacrifice the lives of children to keep me here?"

Oren's expression hardened, and he was more the Oren Darren knew now. "I'm not willing to sacrifice anyone. You are. You're the one setting conditions for helping me. If there's a bad guy here, it's you."

That hurt Darren more than he hoped he let show on his

face. "You have to like me, since you're giving me compliments."

"I don't like you, and you already know that. But this is it. If you want this to happen, this is how it will go. You'll stay with Caley at all times. That means you go to work with him and that you'll be staying at his apartment during the night. Where he goes, you go. Got it?"

Darren nodded. He had no idea what was going on, but he wasn't going to miss this opportunity. "I promise."

Oren rolled his eyes. "I'm not stupid. I know you'll try something even with promises, but I'm ready to risk it to save people."

"That's because you're a better man than I am."

"No one is going to argue that. Ready to leave this cell, then?"

Darren nodded. "More than ready. Where are we going?"

Oren grinned. "You'll see."

Darren didn't trust him as far as he could throw him, which wasn't a lot, considering how much bigger Oren was. Still, when Oren unlocked the door and stepped outside, Darren followed him. He had to. This was his opportunity to get out of the cell, and maybe, if he was lucky, to run away finally. He couldn't if he stayed in the cell, but now that he was going to be out of it, he might have a chance.

He didn't know what he would do if he ran away. Probably go back to his father, even though there was nothing he wanted less. The man was a monster, but he was a monster Darren knew. Darren supposed it was better than nothing.

He followed Oren outside. Oren nodded at the guard waiting there, and the guard followed Darren with his gaze. Darren half expected him to try to stop them, but he didn't say anything, and he and Oren walked away. Darren kept looking around. So far, the only two rooms he'd seen were a cell and interrogation room. He was curious, but there was nothing to see. This was just a big building with a lot of people walking around. Nothing interesting.

"Now that you're out, what can you tell me about the dhampirs?" Oren asked as they walked.

"Not a lot. I've been here for several weeks, which means I'm not in the loop anymore. I can give you a few safehouses, though. They might have relocated, since they know I'm with you, but you could try checking those."

"You're not going to give me anything useful, are you?"

Darren shrugged. "I don't know. I warned you that I didn't have anything useful, since I've been here for a while. You insisted."

"And you took advantage of it."

"Wouldn't you have? I just wanted to get out of the cell."

"You don't deserve to be out of the cell."

Darren agreed, but he didn't say it out loud. "Are you going to go back on your word, then?"

"What do you mean?"

Darren shrugged. "Since I don't have anything useful to give you. Are you going to stick me back in the cell?"

"I'm not. I'm a man of my word. I told you that you would be allowed to stay with Caley, and you will."

Darren was curious about Caley, whoever it was. Oren trusted this man, and he also trusted him to be able to defend himself if Darren tried anything. That was surprising, and it made Darren curious about him.

"Where are we going?" he asked as he noticed they were heading toward the interrogation room.

"You know where. I want to have a chat with you before you meet Caley."

Darren wasn't surprised. "You said I was going to meet your friend."

"And you are. Right after we have another conversation about whatever information you can give me."

"I can only give you a few addresses."

"We'll see."

Darren sighed. It had been too good to be true. He'd thought he was free, at least in part, but instead, he was back in the interrogation room.

He wanted to tell Oren everything. He wanted to explain who his father was, what he'd done, why Darren hated him. He could too easily imagine what would be done to him if he did that, though. Oren already didn't trust him. It would be even worse if he found out that Darren was the dhampir leader's son, which was why Darren couldn't allow anyone to find out about it.

That was one of the few bits of useful information he still had, though. He'd given Oren everything else, but he didn't think Oren believed that. He was going to have to decide whether or not he should tell Oren and risk being killed once he wasn't useful anymore.

Caley, once again standing behind a one-way mirror, watched as Oren and Darren walked into the interrogation room. He was more than happy to listen, mostly because he hoped that Darren would show him that he wasn't making a mistake.

He understood Oren's reasoning. Darren didn't want to be stuck with an enforcer, but Oren needed someone who could defend himself and who wouldn't trust Darren. Most of those people were enforcers, which was exactly the kind of person Darren didn't want to spend time with.

Caley was different, though. He'd been an enforcer once, but not in almost a hundred years. It had become too hard for him, although he supposed that being a medical examiner wasn't any easier. He wanted to continue helping people, and he'd always been interested in science and medicine. He was proud of what he did, but some days, it was hell.

He hoped Darren would be worth it. Oren didn't think Darren had much information he hadn't given them yet, but Caley wasn't too sure about that. He thought Darren was hiding something, although that wasn't surprising. It also didn't make him any less fascinating.

Caley didn't think Darren was a bad guy, not entirely. He was a dhampir, yes, and he'd killed vampires, but he was still a human being with feelings and emotions. Caley was a vampire, but he knew several dhampirs. He knew how hard their lives could be, especially when they were still human and when they first turned. The only way to turn a dhampir into a vampire was through a violent death, and Caley had seen plenty of those on his tables.

That meant that Darren would die of old age, illness, or that he would become a vampire. That alternative wasn't good. Caley had never seen it done, but he knew Oren and the other enforcers killed the dhampirs they captured. When they were sure they wouldn't get any other information from them, they killed them, turning them into vampires. Once that was done, they killed the newborn vampires, too. The dhampirs had to go through two deaths, and while some people believed they deserved it, Caley wasn't one of them.

No one deserved to go through that kind of pain, especially twice. He might make an exception for whoever had killed that little girl, though.

He tightened his hands into fists until he felt the sting of his nails digging into his palms. He wanted to get his hands on whoever had done that and make sure they paid. He wasn't an enforcer anymore, though, and he knew that the best way to help was to stay away from this entire situation. Agreeing to stay with Darren was the best thing he could do right now, which was one of the reasons he had.

The other reason was that he was fascinated with Darren and wanted to get to know him.

He didn't know what he expected or what he wanted, but he supposed he would find out sooner rather than later. He thought Darren was a good person who had been misguided, but he could be wrong, and if that was the case, he would be in trouble. He could defend himself, though, and he knew what to expect from Darren.

Darren and Oren were sitting at the table now, talking. Darren was writing on a piece of paper, and from what Caley could see, he was writing down addresses.

"This is how it works," he was explaining. "The dhampirs are divided into several small groups. All of the groups have a team leader."

"Which was you."

Darren nodded at Oren's words. "It was. The team leaders have only one person to contact to get their orders. I don't know if that person overlooks all the teams or if there's one of them for every single team. I wrote you the name and phone number of the person I got my orders from when I first got here."

"We weren't able to find her."

"I'm not surprised. They give out the orders, but they don't fight. They rely on us to do that."

"And you get killed for it."

Darren grimaced and pushed the piece of paper toward Oren. "We do. You should be happy about that."

"I'm not. The way I see it, you're victims as much as vampires are."

Darren's shoulders went stiff. It was visible even at a distance. "We're not victims. We're dhampirs."

"And whoever is in charge convinces you to work for them, trains you, then sits back and watches the bloodbath. You're weapons for them, nothing more. They're using you, and you don't even see it."

"No one uses me," Darren snapped.

Caley leaned forward. He wanted to go in there and tell Oren to stop, but he knew he couldn't. Oren was trying to get answers, and this was the only way for him to get them.

"All right," Oren said as he raised his hands in surrender. "So you get your orders from this one person. Who gives them to that person, though?"

"I don't know. I already told you that. It's why dhampirs are organized the way they are. By having the team leader talk to only one person, they make sure that we don't know who's in charge or in other teams." He tapped the pen he was still holding onto the table. "That way, if the team is captured, we won't be able to give much information. Which is exactly what happened in this case."

"But you're not just a team leader."

Caley was alarmed by how fast and how much Darren paled. "What are you talking about?" he asked, his voice trembling.

Something was wrong. Caley wanted to go in there and make sure Darren was okay, but he forced himself to stay where he was. Oren wouldn't deny Darren medical help if he needed it, but so far, he'd only paled.

"You know more than what you've been saying. I don't know how you found out, and I don't care. I think you know who's in charge, though."

"Why would you think that?"

"It's the way you've been dancing around the issue, I think."

"So you think I was lying to you just now?"

"I always assume you're lying to me. But no, I think that the way you described it is how dhampirs work."

"We're not just dhampirs. We're vampire hunters. Not all dhampirs want to kill vampires, but all vampire hunters are dhampirs."

Oren waved Darren's words away. "You know what I

mean. Look, if you want to get out of your cell, you're going to have to give me more. I don't know why you keep on hiding it, but it's information I need to stop the dhampirs."

Caley suspected Oren knew why Darren wasn't saying anything else. He was a prisoner and a vampire hunter. He'd realized vampires weren't as evil as he'd thought once he'd spent enough time with them, but that didn't change the fact that he didn't trust Oren or anyone else in this situation. The dhampirs he'd been captured with had been killed. The only one who hadn't been was him, and that was only because he was talking to them. Who was to say that as soon as he gave Oren the last bit of information he knew, Oren wouldn't kill him?

Caley would make sure it didn't happen. Darren wouldn't trust him, either, but Caley would work hard so Darren saw that he could. Darren was a vampire hunter, but that didn't make him a bad person. He was guilty of killing vampires, yes, and it wouldn't be easy for him to get people to trust him, but it didn't mean he couldn't change.

"Give me that piece of paper back," Darren snapped.

"Why? You don't want to give me the addresses anymore?"

Darren stared at Oren for a bit, then shook his head. "I'm just going to add some names to it. Phone numbers. Things like that."

"And who would those names and phone numbers belong to?"

"The people the team leaders answer to. I don't have all the names, and I can't be sure they're alive, or even where they are. It's all I have to give you right now, though."

"We both know that's a lie."

"Yes, well, you're going to have to deal with it, because I'm not telling you anything else. I'm not looking forward to dying. That means I have to make sure you need me, at least for a bit."

Caley stared as the two continued to bicker. This wasn't going to be easy, but he was ready for it. He was useful as the medical examiner, but this was different, and he couldn't wait.

CHAPTER THREE

Darren had no idea what was going on. After he'd answered Oren's questions, Oren had dragged him out of the interrogation room, but not toward his cell. Instead, they were headed toward the building entrance, which made Darren nervous. What was Oren going to do? Was he going to kill Darren now that he knew more? The only bit of information Darren hadn't given him yet was the fact that Darren's father was the head of the dhampirs' organization, and Darren wasn't about to tell anyone. That meant he wasn't useful to Oren anymore, but he hoped Oren didn't realize it.

He swallowed when they stepped into the wide entrance. He was wearing a uniform that was given to all the prisoners, as far as he knew. It certainly got everyone's attention. Everyone turned to look at him, including the receptionist sitting behind his desk. Darren held his head high, turning his attention to Oren so he wouldn't have to see everyone staring.

But Oren wasn't even paying attention to him. He'd taken his phone out, and he was tapping on the screen. He didn't look happy, which made Darren even more nervous.

"Are you ordering an ax?" he asked, trying to lighten the mood.

Oren blinked when he looked up. "I'm sorry?"

"To kill me. What are you doing on your phone? Where are you taking me?"

Oren put his phone away. "You wanted to be out of the cell, didn't you?"

"I did, but this is kind of ominous. I half expect you to kill me."

Oren's lips curled into a wicked smile. "And the other half?"

"Torture."

Oren laughed. "I took a picture of the piece of paper you gave me earlier and sent it to my team. They're already working on it. I should be with them right now."

"And instead, you're babysitting me. You don't have to do it, you know?"

"Nice try. And I won't be babysitting you. Someone else will."

"Are you going to tell me about them, or should I wait until I meet them?"

Oren's smile faded a bit. "I'm going to tell you about him now because I want to warn you."

"He's going to try to kill me?"

Oren shook his head. "No, but *I* am if you do anything to hurt him."

Darren hadn't expected anything different. "I'm listening."

Oren waved at him to continue to follow, and Darren did. He didn't know where they were going, but even though he probably shouldn't, he trusted Oren. If Oren was about to kill him, he would have told him, and he would be handcuffed and surrounded by enforcers. Instead, he was freer than he'd been for several weeks, and it felt good, even though he had no idea what was going on.

"Since you didn't want to stay with an enforcer, I had to find someone else. He's a retired enforcer, so he knows how to defend himself, and he will if you attack him," Oren said as they headed toward the side of the room.

Darren scowled. "I said no enforcers."

"And Caley isn't an enforcer. I just told you. He's retired."

Darren wasn't happy about having to spend time with someone who'd been trained to kick his ass, but he supposed

that retired was better than still working. While his mind offered the image of an older man, Darren knew that probably
wouldn't be the case. If this Caley had been an enforcer, he
had to be a vampire, which meant he wouldn't age. He'd
probably retired because he didn't feel like being an enforcer
anymore, something Darren could fully understand.

"What does he do now, then?" he asked.

Oren's smile came back. "He's our medical examiner."

Darren blinked. "You mean he works with dead people?"

"These days, mostly with the bodies your friends are killing. But yes, that's what he does."

Darren's stomach churned. He couldn't stop thinking
about the little girl the dhampirs had killed. He didn't even
know what she looked like, but it didn't matter. She'd been a
child, and her life had been taken for no reason.

And her body was in this building somewhere, being ex-
amined and taken apart.

Darren swallowed so he wouldn't throw up all over the
place. "Why did he agree to this?"

"In part because he's one of my best friends. I asked him
for a favor, and he agreed to do it for me."

"And the other part?"

Oren opened a door and gestured Darren in.

Darren hadn't known what to expect, but it wasn't a garage
with cars lined up. "For whatever reason, he's fascinated by
you. He wants to get to know you."

"Does he want to open me up and take me apart to see how
I work?"

Oren shrugged. "I'm not sure. You don't have to worry
about that, though. He won't hurt you. He's a good person.
He wouldn't have offered to help you otherwise."

Darren arched a brow. "Did he *actually* offer?"

"Not really, but he did agree, didn't he?"

Darren looked around. "That doesn't explain why we're

here."

"Because while he watched part of the interrogation, he went home after a while. He had a heavy day, and tomorrow is going to be even worse. I told him to get some rest, especially since he's going to have to keep an eye on you."

"Wait. When you said I would have to go to work with him, did you mean I'll have to go to the morgue?"

Oren seemed to find that hilarious. "Exactly. It's where Caley works, so it's where you're going to spend most of your days."

Darren wanted to protest, but he knew better. That was what Oren was waiting for and what he expected. Darren wouldn't have been surprised if Oren had done this on purpose. He wanted Darren to see how many people he and the other dhampirs had hurt, and what better way than having Darren work in the morgue? Even if he didn't have to do anything, he would still have to hang around dead bodies.

He wasn't new to that. He'd killed vampires, and he hadn't thought anything of it. He knew better now, though, and thinking about how many people he'd killed for no reason made him sick. He didn't want to give Oren the satisfaction, though, so when Oren gestured at one of the cars, he climbed into the passenger seat without looking back.

He didn't know what else to do, so he kept his mouth shut as Oren drove them out of the building. He took a deep breath as the warehouse disappeared behind them. He was free, at least in part. He might have to go back to the building and see Oren often enough, but this was better than nothing.

He knew this situation was temporary. Oren wanted someone to keep an eye on him while he used the information he'd given him to find more dhampirs, and hopefully, to run them out of town. It was either that or he and every other dhampir would be killed. Either way, this wouldn't be for long. Darren had never intended it to be.

When he'd said he wanted out of the cell, he hadn't thought about it much, but now, he could see how this was a perfect situation. It would be easier for him to run away now that he was out of the conclave building. Even if he had to come back every day, he wouldn't be spending his entire days there. He knew this Caley guy would keep an eye on him, but he was retired, and he was busy. Surely Darren would find a way to get away from him eventually, maybe even today if he was lucky.

Darren dozed off as Oren drove. Neither of them said anything, which was more than okay with Darren. He jerked awake when Oren parked the car, though, and he looked around. He expected a small house, or maybe a normal-looking apartment building. What was in front of him was nothing like that, though. "Where are we?"

"Caley lives here." Oren left the car, and Darren had to scramble to go after him.

"What do you mean, he lives here?"

"Exactly that. I didn't think you'd have a problem with it."

"I don't." If anything, it made Darren excited at what the next few hours would be like. The apartment building looked like something out of a movie. It was obvious that only people with a lot of money lived in it, which was what had startled Darren.

His eyes went even wider as Oren strode in and nodded at a man standing behind a desk. The man nodded back, then turned his attention to Darren. Oren just waved. "He's with me."

"I won't call up, then, sir."

"There's no need. He already knows we're coming. But thank you, and have a good rest of the night."

Oren and Darren stepped into the elevator. "What was that about?" Darren asked.

"He knows what Caley does for a living. He thinks I'm a

colleague, and he's not wrong."

"None of this makes sense. Why would you want me to stay here?"

"I don't. I already warned you that if you do anything to hurt Caley, I'll make sure it's the last thing you do. Keep that in mind."

How could Darren ever forget it when Oren kept glaring at him?

Caley was nervous. He didn't know why. It wasn't like he had to impress Darren, but still. He wanted the human—the dhampir—to feel at home in his apartment, which didn't make sense. He shouldn't want Darren to come anywhere near him, yet here he was, making sure the pillows on the couch were situated just right and that he had fresh water in the fridge.

A knock on the door made him jerk in surprise. He rushed to open it, smiling when he saw Oren standing there. "You made it."

Oren rolled his eyes. "This isn't a party. I'm just dropping him off. I can't stay long." He eyed Caley. "And you should go to bed. It's almost dawn."

"You shouldn't have forced me to leave the office," Caley grumbled as he stepped aside to let Oren and Darren in.

"Why not? You obviously need rest. You've been over-working yourself in the past weeks, and it's high time you have a good day's rest." He grabbed Darren by the back of the neck and pushed him forward. Darren protested, but Oren ignored him. "Here he is. You're still sure about this?"

Caley nodded. "I am. Besides, it's not like you gave me an alternative."

"I could stick him back in a cell."

"We made a bargain," Darren exclaimed.

"I could have been lying. You are, after all."

Caley cleared his throat. He needed to stop those two before they started fighting in his apartment. "It won't be necessary. You know how upscale security is in this place. I'll make sure he doesn't go anywhere."

"All right. Be careful, and call me if anything goes wrong. I'll be here so fast Darren won't even have the time to think about getting away."

Darren looked like he wanted to prove Oren wrong, but thankfully, he didn't.

Oren glared at him for a moment longer, then nodded and moved toward the door again. "Lock the door as soon as I'm out."

"I will. Thanks for doing this."

Oren snorted and shook his head. "I should be the one thanking you. More importantly, *Darren* should be the one thanking you."

Caley waited until the door closed behind Oren to turn toward Darren. He offered him his hand, and Darren looked down at it as if he didn't quite know what to do with it. "I'm Caley."

"I know. Oren told me."

Caley dropped his hand. This was awkward, but nothing he hadn't expected. "Why don't I give you a tour of the apartment? Or do you want to get takeout first? We can put in an order, then tour the apartment while we wait for it to arrive."

Darren stared at Caley. "Why?"

"Why what?"

"Why are you offering me takeout?"

Caley grinned, making sure to expose his fangs. Darren took a step back, just like Caley had expected. "In case you've forgotten, I'm a vampire. That means I don't have food in the apartment. We can go shopping sometime in the next few days, but this was unexpected, so I don't have anything. It's

44

either takeout, or you don't eat." Caley paused. "Or you could have some of my blood, but somehow, I doubt you'd be happy with it."

Darren grimaced. "Takeout is fine."

It took them a few moments to figure out which restaurants in the area would deliver. There weren't many, considering the late hour of the night, but the options seemed to satisfy Darren, who picked one and made an order. It would take a bit for the food to be delivered, and while they waited, Caley showed him the apartment. "There's not a lot to see. There's the living room, the kitchen, which I don't usually use apart from the fridge, the dining room, and several bedrooms. There's also my office, but I'd like you to stay out of it. I don't take a lot of work home, but I have several sensitive files that you shouldn't see."

"I'll stay away from your office," Darren confirmed. His eyes were wide as he looked around.

Caley went to his bedroom and opened the door. "This is where I sleep."

He pointed at the door on the other side of the hallway. "And this is your guest room." He opened the door and waved Darren inside.

Darren looked around. "This is where I'll be staying?"

"It is. We can go shopping for clothes tomorrow." Caley opened the bathroom door. "You have a separate bathroom, so we don't have to share."

Darren crossed his arms over his chest. "Why are you doing this? You're not just allowing me to stay in this beautiful apartment, but you're talking about buying me food and clothes. Why? It doesn't make sense."

Caley had known he would have to explain. "Well, there's the fact that I'm Oren's best friend. He needed help, and I'm more than happy to provide it, since I can."

"I'm a prisoner. I'm a *killer*. Why would you want me to

stay in your home?"

"I'm a killer, too. I killed people, although most of them when I was an enforcer. But I think that people can change, especially when someone shows them an alternative way to think. I'm also curious about dhampirs."

Baron scoffed. "Of course you are."

"I'm a scientist. I'm sure Oren told you what kind of job I do for the conclave."

Darren grimaced. "He did."

"That's one of the reasons I'm fascinated by dhampirs. They're a meshing of species, and it makes sense that vampires and humans fit together genetically since vampires were once humans. What doesn't is that you have to be killed violently to turn into a vampire. Death is death, however you die. Why would it make a difference?"

"So you want to study me?"

Luckily, Darren didn't look offended. If anything, he appeared amused. "Not exactly. I wouldn't say no if you offered, but I understand that you're a person, and you don't owe me anything."

Darren made a point of looking around. "I think I owe you a lot, actually."

"Don't worry about it. Like I said, I'm taking this as an opportunity."

"An opportunity to do what?"

"To get to know a dhampir. To see the world how you see it, if you're willing to explain. I know this is awkward because I'm a vampire, but it doesn't have to be."

"I'm pretty sure things are awkward because I'm supposed to kill you," Darren pointed out.

"Maybe, maybe not. Do you *want* to kill me?"

"Of course not. I would still be in that cell if it weren't for you."

"And you wouldn't have given Oren the last of the

information. I saw part of the interrogation, so I know what you did."

"You don't know anything about me."

"I suppose I'll find out." Caley didn't know if Darren would allow him to study him, but he wasn't holding his breath. Still, it would be fascinating to spend time with Darren. It was one of the reasons Caley had agreed to this. The other was that he loved Oren and that he wanted to help him.

"You don't know what's going on," Darren murmured.

"You're probably tired. You can go to bed as soon as you're ready."

"I don't know what to think about you or any of this. I feel it's too good to be true."

"Maybe it is, maybe it's not. Maybe I'm doing this because I want even more information, and it's obvious you won't give it to Oren unless something changes."

"So you decided to have me stay in a luxurious apartment?"

"I decided to have you stay with me. Where I live doesn't change that. I'm doing my best friend a favor."

"I hope you won't regret it."

Caley hoped he wouldn't, too. Oren had warned him, and he knew to be careful, but he had no doubt Darren would try to leave eventually. Caley would be ready for it, but in the meantime, he didn't want to think about it too much.

The apartment was quiet. It was dawn, and light peeked through the curtains Darren had closed. He'd always been nocturnal. One had to be, to hunt and kill vampires. It didn't bother him to sleep during the day and fight during the night.

He kept listening, wondering if Caley had gone to sleep. Things had been slightly awkward after the food had arrived for Darren and Darren discovered that Caley intended to eat with him. He hadn't eaten any of the food, of course. He'd taken a bottle from the fridge, and thankfully, it was stainless steel. Darren hadn't seen the blood inside, but the red tinge on Caley's lips had been enough for him to know what it was.

He wasn't surprised. Caley was a vampire, and blood was what he ate. It gave Darren the creeps, but he wouldn't berate Caley for that.

Not anymore.

If he'd still been with the dhampirs, he would have made a fuss. Until recently, he'd still thought vampires didn't deserve to live and that drinking blood was disgusting. He would have stormed out. Now, he realized that blood was the only thing Caley could eat. He didn't have a choice, and it wouldn't be fair for him not to eat just because Darren was there.

So he hadn't said anything, and he'd kept his focus on his own food. The food was good, but then he hadn't expected anything different. Caley was obviously rich, which Darren supposed made sense. He was a vampire, and he'd been a vampire long enough to be an enforcer and retire. He'd no doubt put away money for decades, if not longer, and now he was using it.

Caley wasn't a bad man. Darren hadn't known what to expect, but he'd thought Caley would be like Oren, uncompromising and hard. He was the opposite, though. He'd been honest that he was curious about Darren being a dhampir, but he hadn't pushed for Darren to allow him to examine him or anything like that. He hadn't even brought up the dhampir thing after that first conversation. He'd been acting as if Darren was a friend staying with him rather than a prisoner, and that was confusing.

Why was Caley so nice? It couldn't just be because he was doing a favor for his best friend. He didn't have to be polite and allow Darren to stay in his apartment when Darren was a prisoner, yet he had. And he was gorgeous, too. Both he and Darren were blond, but Caley's hair was curly and looked soft, and Darren wanted to touch it. He hadn't because he liked all his fingers attached, although something in the way Caley looked at him with his big gray eyes told Darren that maybe he wouldn't have disliked it.

But Darren wouldn't be here long enough to find out. Oren had warned Darren that Caley had once been an enforcer, but it had obviously been a while since then, and Caley had gone to bed without hesitation. It meant that Darren would be able to sneak out, which was why he wasn't asleep yet. He was waiting until Caley was unconscious to get to the front door, and now that dawn was here, he knew it wouldn't be long.

He looked around the guest room. He was going to miss this place, even though he'd only been here a few hours. As a dhampir working for his father, he'd never really had a home. Dhampirs moved all over the country, even all over the world sometimes. They didn't have homes. They stayed in motels and abandoned houses, and they had to make do with that. Even the cell Darren had spent so many weeks in had been better than some of the places he'd lived. This apartment beat all of them, though, and he wished he could stay longer.

He knew better.

He got out of bed as silently as he could. He paused every so often to listen, but there was no sound coming from the rest of the apartment. Caley was asleep, which made sense after what Oren had said about him being overworked. With the dhampirs in town, Caley had to have a lot of bodies on his tables. The thought was horrifying, especially so because Darren knew he'd contributed to it. He couldn't think about that right now, though. He had to focus on getting out of here.

He put his shoes on and snuck out of the room. Everything was silent and still, which made it easy for him to listen for Caley. Nothing happened, though, and Darren crept toward the entrance. If he was lucky, he would be out of here in minutes, and away from the apartment not long after.

He felt kind of sorry because Caley was a nice guy. He'd offered Darren a lot when he didn't have to, and Darren was repaying him by sneaking out. Darren shouldn't feel guilty, though. As soon as he was back with the dhampirs, he would have to go back to killing vampires. Eventually, he might even have to kill Caley, and if that happened, he would have to be strong enough to do it. He wouldn't be allowed to think about how nice Caley was, just that he was a vampire and that he should die. He had to get himself back into the right mind-set, no matter how hard it was.

Darren knew his father was in town to get him back. He might not care about Darren as a son, but he did care about him as a dhampir and as the heir to the leadership. People knew who Darren was, so his father wouldn't abandon him with the vampires. He had to make a statement, to show the dhampirs what happened if someone crossed him. This was the best way for him to do that. He would rain violence and blood onto the city until he got what he wanted, which was Darren back under his thumb and all the vampires in the area dead.

Darren finally reached the front door. He paused, listening in, and when he was sure Caley was still asleep and unaware of what was happening, he reached for the front door. He'd seen Caley lock it earlier after the food had arrived, so he knew that the keys were still in the lock.

"I wouldn't do that if I were you," Caley said behind him.

Darren screamed as he whirled around. "What the fuck?"

Caley shrugged. Darren could barely see his expression, but that, he could see. "I said that I wouldn't do that if I were you."

"What are you doing?"

"I think that the question here should be what *you* are

doing. You should be in bed, sleeping, but instead, you're sneaking out."

Darren swallowed. This was it, then. He hadn't managed to leave, and now he would either get beaten to a bloody pulp or marched back to his cell. "Have you already called Oren?"

Caley reached around Darren and flipped on the light. Darren blinked, briefly closing his eyes. "Why would I call Oren?" Caley asked.

"To punish me. I was going to run away."

Caley smiled. "And you don't think both Oren and I expected it? Anyone in your place would have tried. I was surprised you waited so long. I'm kind of sleepy, and I'd like to go to bed."

"You're not angry?"

"I'm not. Oren will be irritated when I tell him tomorrow, but we both expected it. I'm sorry, but I can't let you leave. Even though you're here, you're still a prisoner. The conclave still needs you."

Darren shook his head. "I don't have anything else to give the conclave."

"And even if you did, you wouldn't. I'm not an idiot, Darren. Both Oren and I know you're lying, and we know why. The other dhampirs who were captured with you were killed, and you'll have the same fate unless you have the information we need. That's why you haven't told us everything, and I understand. I won't demand anything from you except that you go back to bed and sleep. Don't try to sneak out again. You wouldn't manage it."

"It's just a door with a lock," Darren pointed out.

"It might be, but I also have a security system. Just because I didn't show it to you doesn't mean it's not there or not active. You should accept it, Darren. You're not going anywhere."

Darren was starting to suspect Caley was right.

Caley had known Darren would try to run. It was what anyone in his place would have done, which was why he'd waited instead of going to sleep. He stood still, waiting for Darren to answer, to tell him whether or not he was going to be nice for the rest of the day and allow Caley to get some rest. When he didn't, Caley asked, "So? Are you going to try to leave again?"

"What would happen if I did?" Darren asked.

"I'll catch you again. You might not think much of me, but I was an enforcer once. I know what I'm doing and how to keep an eye on you." He sighed. "I understand this isn't the best situation for either of us. I don't blame you for wanting to go, even though I know that if you do, you'll eventually kill other vampires. I *will* try to stop you, though. I can't allow you to leave, not when it's my duty to make sure you don't. We can do this the nice way, or I can tie you to the bed until tomorrow."

For whatever reason, Darren seemed amused. "You want to tie me to the bed?"

Caley barked out a surprised laugh. "That's not what I meant, and you know it."

"Maybe I do, maybe I don't." Darren sighed. "All right. I promise I won't try to leave again. I know that you're not as harmless as I thought you were, and I'm not going to risk it, not today. I can't promise I won't try again tomorrow, though, or next week. I'm a prisoner, even though I'm staying in a luxurious apartment."

"I understand that. I hope to change your mind eventually, but if this is all you can give me for now, I'm more than happy to accept it. I just want you to know that I'm not going to hurt you, whatever happens. If you manage to sneak out, I'll just call Oren and tell him what happened."

"And he'll hurt me."

"Only if you don't give him a choice. I know you don't like vampires and that you think we're monsters, but we're not, and Oren isn't a bad person. He's trying to do the best he can, which isn't easy. He wants to protect vampires, and he doesn't quite know what to do with you. He doesn't want to trust you, but he can see you've already changed a lot. He doesn't know what to do with it, and frankly, neither do I. I want to believe all of this, but can I?"

Darren stared for a moment longer.

Caley knew he wouldn't get an answer, so he wasn't surprised when Darren looked away and kept his mouth shut.

Caley sighed. "We should go back to bed, and I mean both of us."

"What if there's a fire?" Darren suddenly asked.

Caley frowned. "What do you mean?"

"Just that. What if there's a fire and I need to be able to leave the apartment? How can I do that if the security system is on?"

Caley rolled his eyes. "You don't have to worry about that. If there's a fire, I'll make sure to get you out of the apartment."

"Or maybe you'll leave me here to die. I'm a dhampir. I killed vampires. No one would blame you for that."

Caley was slightly hurt, but not surprised. "I'm not going to let you die. If there's a fire or anything like that, I promise I'll make sure to get you out of the apartment. It's all I can do. I can't give you the keys or explain how to get around the security system. You know that as well as I do."

"It's not fair. I need to be able to protect myself."

Caley shook his head. "You won't change my mind, so you can stop trying."

Darren glared at him, and Caley half expected him to yell. His eyes widened when instead of doing that, Darren reached for him.

He was ready to fight back, but instead of hurting him, Darren grabbed the collar of his t-shirt, pulled him closer, and kissed him.

Caley was pretty sure his eyes were huge. He hadn't expected this. He didn't know where it was coming from, but he found himself kissing back without even thinking about it.

He liked Darren. He knew Oren would be appalled if he ever found out about this, but he didn't care. Darren was a dhampir, and he'd killed vampires, but he knew how wrong he'd been. He'd been trying to leave, but when he'd been found out, he hadn't turned violent. Most people would have in his place, but instead, he was kissing Caley.

When Darren stumbled back, he looked as surprised as Caley had been. He touched his lips as if he couldn't quite believe what he'd done. Caley waited, wondering what was going to happen next. Darren surprised him in many ways, so he wasn't sure.

"We kissed," Darren said.

Caley chuckled. "You kissed me, if you want to be precise. But yes, we kissed."

"Why?"

"I don't know why you kissed me. That's a question you should be answering, not me."

"I don't know why I kissed you, either."

"I see."

"Do you? Because I don't. I have no idea what's happening."

Caley shook his head. "Nothing has to be happening if you don't want it to. I understand how confusing the situation is, and I won't hold what just happened against you. If you want to act as if nothing happened, we can do that."

Darren stared. "So you would forget all about the kiss?"

Caley grinned. "What kiss?"

Darren shook his head, but he was smiling. "You're not

funny. I'm serious. I have no idea why I kissed you."

"Maybe because you like me."

"I do," Darren confessed.

"But I'm a vampire, and you shouldn't be doing this kind of thing with me."

"Exactly. If the other dhampirs ever find out I kissed you, they would kill me, too."

"They won't find out unless you tell them, and I doubt you're going to. Again, we can ignore what just happened and act as if it hadn't." It would be a pity, because Darren was a great kisser and Caley was attracted to him, but he'd deal with it.

He didn't have relationships. It wasn't because he didn't want to, but rather because he didn't get many opportunities. His job was demanding, and a lot of people were wary of it. He understood why, but it didn't make his love life easier.

Not that he and Darren had a love life. In fact, they were enemies, or at least, they ought to be. Darren hadn't felt like an enemy just now, though.

He was still staring, and Caley stared back.

"It was good," Darren said.

"It was," Caley confirmed.

"I want to do it again."

"I wouldn't stop you."

"You should."

"And you shouldn't be kissing me. What are you going to do about it?"

As an answer, Darren reached for Caley again. He dragged him closer, and this time, Caley wrapped his arms around Darren's neck. When Darren kissed him, Caley plastered their bodies together.

If they were going to do this, they ought to do it right.

"This is crazy," Darren murmured against Caley's lips.

"Is it a problem?"

"Not at the moment, no." He kissed Caley again, and Caley decided they'd both talked enough for the night.

He continued kissing Darren, but at the same time, he started pulling him toward the hallway that led to the bedrooms. He wasn't about to do this in the entrance, even though no one would find them. Darren didn't protest, but he did hesitate when they stumbled into Caley's bedroom — although that might be because Caley had finally managed to unzip Darren's pants, and they'd fallen to his ankles.

"This is crazy," Darren panted.

"Do you care? No one has to know." Caley wasn't sure why he wanted this so much, but it had been so long since he'd last felt this close to another man, and he wasn't about to give it up just because Oren would wring his neck if he ever found out.

"It could get both of us killed."

"It could also get both of us off." Caley kissed Darren hard. "We can stop if you want, but I don't, and I don't think you do, either."

Darren hooked an arm around Caley's waist and pulled him closer. "You're right."

"I usually am." Then Caley stopped being smug because Darren kissed him again.

They tried moving toward the bed, but Darren stumbled. He glared down at his feet, where his pants were tangled. Caley dropped to his knees, more than ready to get Darren naked. He helped Darren get rid of his shoes and socks, then his pants. When all that was left on his lower body was his underwear, Caley hooked two fingers under the waistband at Darren's hips and looked up in question.

Darren was hard under the thin fabric, his cock straining to burst out. Caley couldn't wait to get his hands — or his mouth — on it, but he didn't want to do anything Darren would be uncomfortable with.

Darren nodded, though, and Caley tugged the underwear down, revealing him. He pressed his nose where Darren's thigh met his groin and took a deep breath, closing his eyes. He loved this. He loved the scent of man, of sex, and knowing that soon they would be naked together. First he wanted to take care of Darren. He didn't know Darren's back story, but something told him it wasn't a nice one and that not a lot of people took care of him and showed him he deserved it.

He didn't want to tease Darren more than he already had, so as he lifted his head, he licked along Darren's cock. Darren groaned and staggered, but Caley was strong enough to hold him up. He wanted Darren to rely on him and stop thinking about running away.

He wanted Darren to stop thinking, period.

He wrapped his lips around the head of Darren's cock and gently sucked as he slid the tip of his tongue over the slit. It tasted bitter and salty, which was satisfying in its own right, even though it wasn't Caley's favorite thing to taste. It told Caley that Darren was enjoying this, which was what he was aiming for.

He sucked harder, dancing his tongue up and down Darren's cock as he lowered and raised his head. He felt fingers touching the top of his hair and would have grinned if his mouth hadn't been otherwise occupied. It was, though, so he focused on what he was doing and on giving Darren as much pleasure as he could.

"You're going to make me come," Darren warned.

Caley continued, since that was kind of the point.

"I want you to come, too. Come on, Caley. Let's get on the bed."

Caley let go of Darren's cock with a pop. "I thought you wanted to come."

Darren reached down and helped him to his feet. His cock was slick with saliva, and Caley wanted to suck on it until

Darren filled his mouth with his pleasure. He wanted to drink him down, which wasn't something he did with his few one-night stands.

But Darren wasn't just a one-night stand, as he showed when he kissed Caley without hesitation. "I do want to come, but not alone. We're doing this together, not just me."

It seemed like every time Darren said or did something, Caley found more proof that he wasn't the bad person everyone assumed he was.

He kissed Darren again, and they finally stumbled toward the bed. Darren was half-naked already, but luckily Caley was wearing pajamas, which meant a t-shirt and soft pants.

When Darren reached inside the pants and found that Caley wasn't wearing underwear, he arched a brow, but he didn't say anything about it. Instead, he pushed Caley's pants down, exposing him, and pressed harder against him.

Caley hissed when their cocks brushed against each other. He needed more, and he needed it now.

He rolled to his side, or at least, he tried to. Darren leaned back, frowning, but Caley shook his head and got into position after whipping his t-shirt off. He turned his back on Darren, then twisted to look at him. "Come on."

He didn't have to ask twice. Darren finished getting naked, too, and slotted himself behind Caley, pressing his chest against Caley's back. They had to maneuver a bit to get his cock between Caley's thighs, but once he settled, it was heaven.

Darren wasn't a selfish lover. As soon as he started moving his hips, he also wrapped his fingers around Caley's cock. He used the same rhythm with his body and his hand, and Caley had to screw his eyes shut so he wouldn't embarrass himself and come all over Darren's hand too soon.

It wasn't going to take long, though. The head of Darren's cock brushed against the base of Caley's balls every time he moved, sending whispers of pleasure to Caley's groin. The pressure and movement on his cock were near perfect, and while he wished he was kissing Darren, he wasn't willing to stop.

Then Darren bit Caley's neck. Caley hadn't expected it, and he cried out, tipping right into his orgasm. He heard Darren chuckle as he thrust harder against him, and he reached back, squeezing Darren's ass cheek. Darren grunted and buried his face against Caley's neck. Caley felt his damp lips and the flick of a tongue, then finally, the warm stickiness of Darren's seed as he came between his thighs.

They lay there, panting. Caley's eyes were open, but he felt the moment Darren slid into sleep. They hadn't even cleaned up, but he didn't care.

He didn't know what tomorrow would be like, whether Darren would freak out over having sex with a vampire or biting one, but for now, he allowed himself to bask in the feeling of someone holding him as he let sleep take over.

CHAPTER FOUR

Darren was going to run away. Really, he was.
Eventually.

He was only waiting for the right opportunity. He still remembered the night when Caley had found him while he'd
been trying to sneak out of the apartment. He didn't want to
go through that again. If he left, no one could see him.

He glared at the white wall in front of him. He was at work
with Caley, but he refused to go inside the morgue, and Caley
was more than okay with that. He didn't want anyone who
shouldn't be there to be around, just in case they did something they shouldn't, which in Darren's case, everyone expected to happen. Darren wouldn't go in even if someone
paid him, which he was pretty sure Oren was tempted to do,
just to see what would happen. Darren would never do something that would make Caley unhappy, though.

Okay, so Darren wasn't just staying because he was looking for the perfect opportunity to leave. That was part of it,
but only a small portion. The main reason he was still here
was that he didn't want to leave Caley behind.

It was strange. Darren wasn't used to the liberal affection
Caley showed him. Dhampirs' lives were hard and bloody,
and there was no love in them. Even the couples Darren had
seen were cold with each other. It looked more like they were
together for convenience than because they loved each other,
but being with Caley was different.

Darren wouldn't call what they had love, not yet, and
maybe not ever, but it was enough to keep him here. Of

course, it didn't take much to keep him away from his father. The man was a monster, and as soon as he got his hands on Darren again, he would make sure Darren knew how angry he was that vampires had captured his son. Darren wasn't even sure his father would allow him to explain. Not only had Darren been captured, but he was still alive, and he was being treated well. Everyone would think him a traitor, and Darren wouldn't blame them.

He *was* a traitor.

That thought was enough to make him panic, even though he knew he was doing the right thing. He'd helped Oren as much as he was ready to, and hopefully, it would be enough to slow down the dhampirs. It wouldn't stop them, because nothing could, but maybe they would stop killing human children to get what they wanted. It wasn't right, but then when had a dhampir's decision been right?

Darren sighed and rubbed his face. For the first time in his life, he was getting regular sleep and food. He felt better physically than he had in a long time, maybe ever, and he didn't want to lose that.

He also didn't want to lose Caley.

Darren didn't know what he'd been thinking when he'd first kissed Caley, but he didn't regret it. He couldn't, not when it had given him so much. Staying in Caley's apartment didn't have anything to do with their relationship, but everything else did. Caley kissed and cuddled Darren any time he felt like it, and Darren never quite knew how to answer. He wasn't used to it, but he could see himself doing this for years to come. He was human, but he knew Caley didn't care. He also wouldn't suggest that Darren be turned into a vampire. He knew how much Darren feared it, and he seemed quite content to continue the way they had been.

It hadn't been long, though, and things might change. They *would* change eventually, and when they did, Darren would have to go. What would he go back to, though? The more time that passed, the better he looked physically, the higher the chances he was a traitor. There was no way he would be welcome back with open arms, not even by his father—especially not by him. He would know what had happened, at least in part, and he would make sure Darren paid.

"I thought I told you that you had to go to work with him," a voice said.

Darren jerked so hard that he hit the back of his head against the wall behind him. He scowled at Oren, who looked satisfied. "I *am* at work with him."

Oren looked at Darren, then at the door that led into the morgue. "He's in there, and you're out here in the hallway. You're not at work with him."

"Only because he doesn't want me to go inside, and you know it. He doesn't even want *you* to go inside unless he has something to show you."

Oren stared at Darren for a moment.

Darren had no idea why, but Caley trusted him enough that he didn't have a problem with Darren staying out here in the hallway while he worked. He seemed convinced that Darren wouldn't try to leave, and so far, Darren hadn't. There was no point, not when he was in the conclave building. Anyone who saw him would know who he was and what he was doing, so there was no point trying to escape.

Oren looked like he wanted Darren to try, though. He probably wouldn't hesitate to beat Darren up if he as much as moved toward the front door on his own.

"I'm keeping an eye on you," Oren eventually said.

Darren rolled his eyes. "You think I don't know that? You've been this dark shadow over my shoulder ever since I met you."

Oren grinned. "As long as you know it." He stopped in front of the morgue door and knocked quickly.

Darren had been here long enough to know that the knock would be enough for Caley to know who was there. "What do you need from him?" he asked.

Oren arched a brow. "Why do you want to know?"

Darren couldn't tell him it was because he was falling in love with Caley and wanted to protect him, even from Oren. "Just curious," he answered, trying to look as if he didn't really care.

He did, probably too much. *Definitely* too much. The fact that he was falling in love with Caley, with a *vampire*, was a disaster. He couldn't find it in himself to stop, though. He wanted Caley in his life, even though he knew it wouldn't be for long. He supposed he was trying to make the most of what little time he and Caley had.

The morgue door opened, and Caley came through, along with cold air and the smell of bleach, blood, and death. He was wearing scrubs, but not all the other stuff he put on when he performed an autopsy. There was no sign of blood on him, which was a relief.

He smiled at Oren, but his gaze moved on to Darren right away, and Darren wasn't surprised when Caley made a beeline for him and kissed him. "Was I too long?" Caley asked.

Darren shook his head. "Don't worry about me. I know you have work."

"You should bring a book next time."

"I will."

"Are you two done?" Oren asked. He didn't sound angry, but he did sound wary and puzzled.

Darren understood. If anyone had told him a few weeks ago that he was going to be in a relationship with a vampire, he would have told them they were mad. He wouldn't have believed it, and sometimes, he still had a hard time believing it even though he actually *was* in a relationship with Caley.

It felt like a dream, like all of this wasn't his life, and he supposed it wasn't, not like his normal life as a vampire hunter. His father would have a heart attack if he saw Darren right now, and right that, he would try to kill Darren.

Was that really what Darren wanted to go back to? Did he actually have a reason to run away? When he thought about the life he'd left behind, he could see how bad it had been. He'd been brainwashed into thinking all vampires were evil. He'd been pushed into killing people who hadn't deserved it. He'd been made a murderer, and he'd been too stupid to doubt what was said to him. He'd been too afraid to question his father, but now he knew better.

Just like humans, not all vampires were evil, and not all of them were killers. Even if some had killed, it was usually because they'd had to, or because like Oren, they were trying to defend other people. That didn't make them bad, not like the vampire hunters, who were actively killing innocent vampires.

Darren didn't know if he could go back to that, but he was going to have to make a decision, and fast.

"What did you need?" Caley asked Oren.

"To talk to you for a moment about the last victims."

Caley grimaced. "Of course. Do you want to go to my office?"

Oren's gaze slid to Darren, who seemed lost in his thoughts. "I think it's better if we do, yes."

Caley knew he was about to be dragged into a conversation about Darren. He wasn't looking forward to it, but he'd known it was coming since the first time he'd come to work and had kissed Darren in front of everyone.

It had been the day after they'd made love, when they'd woken up together in Caley's bed. Darren had been awkward, but Caley had tried to reassure him. He didn't expect Darren to go back to his own bed or to act like nothing had happened. He didn't care what other vampires thought. He was an adult, had been for a long time, and he would make his own decisions. If one of those decisions was to be in a relationship with a dhampir vampire hunter, then so be it. He'd been surprised Oren hadn't dragged him into an office and yelled at him that first day, but he supposed it had only been delayed.

He sighed and turned his attention back to Darren. "I'm done with the autopsy, so once this meeting is over, we can go to the cafeteria."

That finally got a smile out of Darren. "I don't think I want anything you guys sell in there."

Caley grimaced, remembering well how Darren had reacted to that first time they had. "I made sure they had some human food for you. I don't know what it will be, so I hope it won't be disgusting, but it won't be blood. Or we can grab something before going back to the apartment."

Darren's expression twisted. "You shouldn't have done that."

"Done what?" Caley asked.

"Made things easier for me. I don't understand why you're doing it."

"We'll have that conversation later, all right?" He leaned closer and kissed Darren's cheek. "But I'm doing this because I care about you," he murmured. He leaned back without giving Darren the time to answer. He wasn't sure he wanted to find out what Darren thought about him.

As far as he knew, he was only convenient. He and Darren lived together right now, and they spent most of their days together when Caley wasn't in the morgue. No one else in the building wanted to spend any time with Darren, except for Falkner, but he had his own life, and Oren, who only wanted information.

Caley was different. It had been easy for them to slide into a relationship, and Caley couldn't help but wonder how easy it would be for them to slide out of it, too. He knew he had growing feelings for Darren, but he couldn't tell whether Darren shared those feelings.

He looked at Oren, gesturing at the morgue doors. "Let's go in, then."

Oren grimaced but nodded. Of course, he couldn't leave without talking to Darren one last time. "I want to see you here when I'm done."

Darren grinned at him. "Where do you think I would go? I'm stuck here, remember?"

"As long as *you* remember it."

Oren pushed open the morgue door and walked through. With one last glance at Darren, Caley followed him. "Do you really have to antagonize him every opportunity you have?" he asked as he and Oren walked to his tiny office.

"Why wouldn't I? He's a dhampir, a vampire hunter. He kills vampires for a living, Caley."

"I'm very much aware of that, thank you."

"Why did you kiss him, then? What are you doing?"

Caley closed the door to his office and moved around his desk. "Because we're sleeping together."

Oren made a strangled noise. "I was hoping that wasn't the case. What are you thinking?"

"That I like him, and that he's hot. He's also good in bed, by the way."

Oren sat on the other side of the desk and shook his head. "I do *not* want any details about that."

"Good, because I don't want to give you any details."

"You know who he is, though. You know what he did. How can you trust him?"

Caley wasn't sure how to answer that question. Oren already knew what he thought of Darren, and it had nothing to do with the fact that they were sleeping together.

He liked Darren, and he was convinced that deep inside, Darren didn't want to hurt anyone. From the little Darren had said from his past life, he'd grown up in the vampire hunter business. He'd been manipulated into it, told it was the only right thing he could do. If one had been told their whole life that someone else was evil, wouldn't it make sense for them to try to kill them? Besides, the vampire hunters were a group, a vast family, even though they were a family who didn't like each other. They gave Darren a sense of belonging that he didn't have with anyone else.

He never talked about his family, or even whether or not he had one. Caley had concluded that apart from the hunters, he didn't. If he lost the hunters, he'd be alone in the world, and it was obvious he didn't want that to happen. Who would?

Oren shook his head. "I don't know what he told you, but you can't trust him."

"I wish you'd trust me."

"I do. I also believe that he's going to betray you, though. He's sneaky. What's to say that he's not sleeping with you so you relax and don't see him planning on running away?"

"I might be retired, but I'm not an idiot." And Caley didn't entirely trust Darren. He knew that Darren was still planning to run away, even though he hadn't yet. Maybe he didn't want to anymore, not now that they were together.

Caley wanted to trust Darren. He wanted to see what could happen between them, how Darren could become part of his life. He would never ask Darren to turn into a vampire, since he knew how much Darren loathed the idea, but Darren was young. They could have many decades together. They could be happy.

Caley wasn't sure it would ever happen. "So, what do you want to know about the case?" he asked.

Oren stared at him for a moment. "That's all you have to

say about your relationship with him?"

"What I have to say is that it's none of your business. I know who Darren is and what he did. I know the risks. You trusted me with him before, and you're going to have to continue."

"I'm worried about you."

"You shouldn't be. I'm perfectly fine."

"We both know that's not the truth, but fine. If you want to act as if everything is perfect, we will, at least for a bit." He paused before asking, "What can you tell me about the family that was killed, then?"

Caley had known this was why Oren was here, so he'd gotten the reports ready. He handed them to him, quickly going over them just in case there was something Oren didn't understand. When they were done, he was exhausted. He didn't walk out with Oren, though. He gave him time to leave, no doubt after bickering with Darren for a bit. Then he followed him outside.

Darren was waiting there, sitting on the floor. He scrambled to his feet as soon as he saw Caley, and Caley grimaced. "I'll make sure there's a chair for you tomorrow."

"You don't have to. I'm fine sitting on the floor."

"It can't be comfortable."

"It's not, but it's something I'm used to. Are we going to the cafeteria, or are we headed home?"

The fact that Darren called Caley's apartment *home* made Caley's chest tighten. He and Darren were sleeping together, but they weren't in a relationship, even though Caley wanted to be. They hadn't talked about it, but maybe Caley could do something to hint at it without actually having a conversation. "Actually, I thought we could go out."

Darren blinked. "Out?"

"On a proper date."

Darren had no idea what to think of that. "A date?"

"I know what we have is nebulous. We haven't talked about it, and you probably don't want to. I think it would be nice for us to get something to eat together. If you don't want to, though, it's perfectly fine, too."

"How would it work? You said we could eat together, but I'm not about to start drinking blood."

Caley smiled. "Is that you saying yes if I can find a way around it?"

Darren hesitated only for a moment. "It is." He was looking forward to going on a date with Caley. He knew it was probably stupid, but he couldn't stop himself. He didn't know how long he still had with Caley, and he wanted to make the most of it.

"So you trust me?"

To Darren's own surprise, he did. "I do. Lead the way."

He didn't know what to expect, but he trusted Caley enough to know he wouldn't be in danger. He trusted Caley enough to sleep next to him in a bed, to be unconscious with him. He knew Caley would never hurt him or try to turn him. That wasn't the kind of person Caley was.

Darren's father would have called him a fool and an idiot, and maybe he would have been right. Caley seemed perfect, though, and Darren couldn't find it in himself to care about what his father would think about him.

His father already believed Darren was an idiot anyway. This wouldn't change anything. It would give him one more reason to kill Darren, but then, he already had a long list of them.

"I'm sure you're not aware of it, but there are places in the city that cater to both vampires and humans," Caley explained once they were in the car.

"Really?"

"Really. Vampire-human relationships are more common than you think. Some humans fear us, of course, but not all of them do, and I've had relationships with humans in the past." He paused. "And right now, of course."

"Why do you do it? Isn't it horrible when a human starts to age and dies? Or do you turn all your lovers?"

Caley looked horrified. "I don't. I don't think any vampire does. Sometimes, the relationship ends like a normal relationship between humans would. Sometimes, they last, and we have to watch the people we love die. It's a fact of life, though, and we deal with it."

"Why would you want to do that? Why would you want to go through the pain?"

Caley's smile was sad. "Because love is worth it. What's life without love?"

"Having a boyfriend isn't everything."

"I don't mean only lovers. I also mean friends, family. We can't turn everyone we love. A lot of people would never want to be vampires, just like you. It's not something that should be forced on you, even though some vampires do it. I think it's despicable, even though, in a way, I can understand. I've lost family and lovers, and I miss them, but I wouldn't change what we had."

"So the same would go for me?"

"If our relationship continues, sure. I know you never want to be turned, and I respect that. I didn't want to be turned, either. I learned to deal with it, and it's not so bad now that I'm settled, but I understand how hard it can be. I know what it's like to hate yourself for what you've become, for what you have to do to survive, and for not being able to kill yourself."

It was Darren's turn to be horrified. "You tried to kill yourself?"

"It was a long time ago, right after I was turned. Like you, I thought that since I was a vampire, I was a monster. I know that wasn't the case now, and I'm happy I failed."

"I'm happy, too."

The conversation lagged after that. Caley had given Darren a lot to think about, and Darren needed to wrap his mind around everything. They stayed silent until Caley parked the car and guided Darren toward the restaurant he'd chosen. Darren was distracted until they reached it.

His eyes were wide as they walked in, though. He didn't know what to expect, so he kept looking around while Caley guided him with a hand on the small of his back. He nodded at the maître d', who seemed to know him, and took them straight to what had to be the best table in the restaurant.

Darren was surprised to find menus on the table. He gingerly took the one in front of him after sliding into his seat, then opened it. He didn't know what to expect, but it wasn't the shortlist of pasta dishes, meat, and fish. "There's human food in here."

"There is. I told you, this restaurant has both vampire and human customers, usually together, of course. It's hidden by magic so humans who aren't in the know can't stumble onto it. Once they know about it, though, they can come back."

"What about you? You're just going to order blood?"

Caley tapped the menu in front of him, which was different from Darren's. "As you can see, they have several different types."

Darren grimaced. "Do I want to know?"

"You don't have to if you don't want to. But yes, I'll order blood. Don't worry. I won't make a mess."

Darren was always wary when Caley ate, and he made sure not to look at him as he did so. Eventually, though, he was going to have to be more comfortable with it if they were going to continue whatever it was they were doing. Caley shouldn't have to hide his food or what he was. He was trying to be considerate for Darren, and Darren disliked himself for that need.

He took a deep breath and looked at Caley's menu. "Can I see that?"

Caley's brows shot up his forehead. "Are you sure?"

Darren wasn't, but he nodded. "I'm sure."

Caley handed him his menu, and Darren looked down at it. It was much shorter than the human one, but it still had choices. There were all kinds of human blood—A, B, AB, and O—but also different kinds of animal blood. "I didn't know vampires drank animal blood."

"It's not ideal, but we can, yes. It's a bit like humans drinking alcohol, although without the secondary effects. We can drink it, and we can even like it, but it's not as nutritious as human blood."

Darren grimaced. That was too many details he didn't want to know. He decided to move the conversation to another topic. "So you never wanted to be turned?"

Caley shook his head. "I didn't, no. I didn't even know vampires existed before I was." He paused when the waiter came toward them. Darren hadn't chosen his food, so he picked the first thing he saw on the menu, ordering a steak with a baked potato.

Caley continued once they were alone again. "As I suspect you know by now, I'm rich. In part, it's because I've been a vampire for a while, and I know how to invest my money. Mostly, though, it's because my parents were rich. I was their only heir, and when they died, everything went to me."

"Even though you were a vampire?"

"Even though I was a vampire, yes. They knew, of course. After I was turned, we had to take precautions. I couldn't go in the sun or to dinner with other people. We made it work, and it's thanks to them that I didn't kill myself. They showed me that even though I was different, I still deserved their love."

Darren was touched, and he couldn't help but imagine what his life would have been like if his father had been more like Caley's parents. "My father hates me."

Caley frowned. "Why?"

"He thinks I'm not enough. He's a hunter. He always was, and he was the one who taught me how to hunt. He was always tough on me, even when I was a child." Darren had never told anyone. No one in his life would have cared — until Caley.

"I see. Well, I think he's wrong. You're strong, Darren, much stronger than you seem to think."

Darren wasn't sure he believed Caley, but he wanted to, very much so. "I don't know about that."

"I do. I think it takes a lot of strength to do what you did."

"What do you mean?"

"You admitted you were wrong. You didn't hide your head in the sand, and you got to know vampires. That's how you realized that not all of us are bad people. Not all of us are killers, not cold-blooded killers anyway. You allowed us to change your mind, and it takes a lot of strength to admit that you were wrong."

Darren could see Caley was convinced of what he was saying. He wanted Darren to be a good person, but Darren really wasn't. He was going to break Caley's heart eventually, and he already hated himself for it.

Caley already knew Darren didn't hate him. He wouldn't be sleeping with him otherwise. He hadn't been sure what Darren felt for him, and now he knew, at least in part. Darren didn't believe Caley deserved to die, even though he was a vampire. Whether or not he'd ever truly believed all vampires should be dead, he didn't anymore.

Caley knew he was taking a risk by choosing this

restaurant, but he wanted to show Darren what they could have. He wanted to show him that not all vampires killed humans for their blood. Only a small number did, and they'd given vampires a bad reputation. He wanted that reputation to change, but it was going to take a lot of time and effort.

He was sad and angry about Darren's life as a child, but he wasn't surprised. He'd suspected something like that had happened to Darren and that it was the reason Darren hated vampires so much. It was something that had been taught to him. He wasn't sure whether or not Darren would answer his questions, but he wouldn't find out if he didn't try. "Can I ask about your mother?" She had to have been a vampire, which didn't make sense, given what Caley knew about Darren's father.

Darren looked away and shrugged. "I never knew her. She left when I was a baby. My father said that as soon as I was born, she went away and never came back."

"And you believed him?"

Darren jerked back. Apparently, he'd never thought about the fact that his father could easily have lied to him. "Of course I did. Why wouldn't I?"

"I understand why you did when you were younger. But now, you know your father was wrong when it comes to vampires."

"Not all of them."

"Not all of them, no," Caley agreed. "But we're like humans. Some of them are killers, but most aren't. The same goes for vampires, especially these days. It's much easier now to find blood freely given. We don't even have to meet the humans who gave it."

"You think my father lied to me."

"I think he might have, yes. You said that he's always hated vampires as long as you can remember. Why would he have had a relationship with one?"

"Maybe he started hating vampires because of my mother."

"I suppose it's a possibility." But Caley highly doubted it. It seemed to him that Darren's story had a lot of holes, but neither of them could fill them. "Would it be so bad, though?"

"Would what be so bad?"

"To be a vampire. I understand you dislike the idea because you've been taught that vampires are evil. Turning into one has to be the worst thing you can think of. I'm a vampire, though, and I've never hurt anyone." Not anyone who hadn't tried hurting him first, anyway.

"God, no. I never want to be a vampire. I can't think of anything worse, just like you said."

"That's the old you talking. *Now* you know that being a vampire doesn't mean you're a bloodthirsty monster. Look at me. You don't seem to have a problem sleeping with me, even though I could bite you at any second."

Darren's cheeks turned slightly red. It was delightful. "It's because I trust you. I know you would never bite me, not unless I asked you to." He looked at Caley in the eyes. "And I'm never going to. No offense, but I'm not comfortable with it."

Caley arched a brow. "You don't seem to have a problem biting me, though."

The red on Darren's cheeks deepened. He looked away, but he was smiling. "I never really think about it before I do it. I can stop, if you want me to."

"Don't. I enjoy it as much as you do. But you're right. I would never bite you unless you agreed to it. That's not what we're talking about, though. You know that it would be fairly easy for you to turn into a vampire. What would you do if it happened?"

Darren took his time answering. As he did, the waiter came back with their meal. Caley nodded at him and turned his attention to his blood, hoping Darren wouldn't have a problem with it. So far, he didn't seem to be bothered, but they'd only eaten at Caley's apartment.

"I understand what you're saying," Darren finally said after he'd eaten some of his steak. "Not all vampires are monsters, just like not all humans are good people. God knows that my father is a monster, even though he's a dhampir."

"He is?" Caley hadn't known that bit of information, and he found it interesting.

Darren nodded, but he seemed lost in his thoughts. "I understand all that, but the thought of becoming a vampire horrifies me. Logically, I know it wouldn't change me. I know that while I would have to drink blood and wouldn't be able to go out in the sun, I would still be me."

"But emotionally, you've been told that being a vampire was as good as being a killer, and of course, you don't want that."

Darren snorted. "Which is ironic, considering the fact that I'm already a killer. It wouldn't make me a monster, though."

"It wouldn't, no."

Darren hesitated. "How is it? I know it wouldn't be the same for me as it was for you since I'm a dhampir, but I'm curious."

Caley always did his best not to think about when he'd been turned, but he didn't mind as much if it was for Darren. "It was painful. I tried to fight it, and the vampire who turned me made sure I would feel all of it. I think he enjoyed the pain and fear. The act itself was terrible, as was not understanding what was happening to me. Being a vampire isn't that bad, though. You get used to it after a while."

"It has to be strange, though. You have to leave your entire life behind."

"That's not true. I thought I would have to once I realized what I was. That's when I tried to kill myself. I didn't want to tell my parents that I'd become a monster. They found me,

though, and they stopped me. When I told them what I'd become, they were shocked, but they told me it didn't change
the way they felt about me. They loved me. They wanted me
to be happy, and we worked toward that." Caley looked at
Darren. "I want you to be happy, too, whatever that means
for you."

Darren shook his head. "Why? I'm a hunter. I could kill
you easily. I know we're sleeping together, but it doesn't
change what I am."

"It also doesn't change *who* you are, which is a good person."

"I don't know how you can think that of me."

Caley reached over the table to take one of Darren's hands.
He squeezed, and Darren smiled softly. "You've made mis-
takes. Everyone does."

"Killing innocent people isn't exactly a mistake."

"Not a mistake, then. But you were misguided. Your father
is the only family you ever had, and you've always wanted to
make him proud. You also never doubted what he was telling
you, not until recently."

"I should have known better."

"Maybe, maybe not. How could you have known better if
you never knew anything else? You told me yourself that you
grew up surrounded by hunters. Getting away from that is
impressive."

"It only happened because Oren captured me."

"Even so. You could have refused to talk. You could have
stayed stubborn and been killed with the other dhampirs you
were brought in with. Instead, you realized that what you
knew was wrong, and you decided to help."

"You know I'm still hiding something."

Caley squeezed harder. "I'm aware of that, yes. Oren is,
too. I hope that eventually, you'll tell me whatever is still on
your mind. Even if you never do, though, it doesn't matter.

You've done everything you could to help us, even though we're vampires. You know that what your father and the other hunters are doing is wrong. You could have run away from me several times in the past few days, but you didn't. You didn't even try, and to me, that's telling."

Darren blushed. "What does it tell you?"

"Well, that you like me, but more importantly, that you realize how wrong you and your father were, and that you're ready to make a change."

"I don't know if I can."

"You already have. Change isn't easy, but you've already done the hard part."

Darren clearly didn't believe Caley, so Caley dropped it. He could already tell that Darren's father was going to be a problem. Something Darren had said made Caley wonder if his father had been lying to him all his life.

The man was a dhampir. He knew what being a dhampir meant, yet he'd had a child with a vampire. Why? If he hated being a dhampir so much, why had he wanted to bring another one into the world?

CHAPTER FIVE

Okay, so maybe Darren *wasn't* going to run away after all. He'd barely thought about it since the first time he'd tried, and since he and Caley had gotten together, he didn't *want* to think about it.

His father would kill him with his bare hands if he ever found out about this, but Darren didn't care. He could see him and Caley having something in the long run. It would be strange to age next to Caley when Caley wouldn't age, but Darren thought he could wrap his mind around it and get used to it. Caley certainly didn't seem to have a problem with it.

He'd never mentioned turning Darren, not beyond asking him if it would be so bad to be a vampire when they'd gone on their first official date. Darren had been clear, and Caley had accepted his decision. He wouldn't try to convince him, and Darren was relieved.

He understood that being a vampire wasn't bad. He knew he would still be himself, that he wouldn't turn into a blood-thirsty monster just because he wasn't human anymore. He couldn't seem to let go of the horror that the thought of being turned caused in him, though. Maybe in time he would get used to it, but he was more than happy to stay human right now.

"How is it?" Caley asked.

Darren looked down at his sandwich. It wasn't great, but then, he hadn't expected it to be. He'd been surprised when Caley had told him that he'd asked the conclave, or rather, the people in charge of the cafeteria in the conclave building, to make sure he had human food available. He couldn't believe Caley had thought about it and gone through with it. "It's great."

Caley eyed him above his stainless-steel bottle. "You're lying."

Darren made a show of taking a bite of his sandwich. "I'm not," he said once he'd swallowed the bite.

"I know you are. I can tell."

"How?"

Caley tapped the skin next to his eye. "You squint a bit when you're lying. I noticed it the first time I watched one of your interrogations."

"You mean when Oren threatened to hurt me if I didn't tell him everything I knew?"

That made Caley laugh. "You mean he only did it once? But yes, that's how I know you have more to tell him and how I know you're lying now. If the sandwich isn't good, I can ask them to get something else, or we could bring something from home."

"The sandwich is fine. It's not high cuisine, but I can deal with it. Trust me. I've had much worse."

Caley grimaced and reached over the table for Darren's hand. "The fact that you had worse doesn't mean you should have it now, too. It doesn't mean you don't deserve more."

Darren was touched, but he wasn't surprised. Caley had been taking care of him since that first day, and he wasn't giving any sign that he would stop. Darren was glad. He still wasn't sure how they could work together, since he was a dhampir, and more importantly, a vampire hunter, while Caley was a vampire. He supposed they would find out eventually.

It wouldn't be easy, but then, nothing worth having was easy. He'd found that out the hard way.

He wanted this to work. He'd never thought he would have it — that he would have a relationship, that he would be loved for who he was and not for what he could do. Not that his father had ever loved him. His father loved what Darren could do, what he could become, but he'd never been happy with what Darren actually was.

Darren had never been enough for his father, but he *was* enough for Caley, and that made him fall in love with Caley a little bit more every time he realized it. Caley had never said the words, but he didn't have to. It was in every move he made, every word he told Darren.

Darren couldn't believe how lucky he'd been. All the other dhampirs captured with him had been killed, yet here he was, basically free, with a best friend and a boyfriend. He had no idea what he'd done to deserve all of this, but he had to come clean with Oren, and more importantly, with Caley. He'd been lying to them by not telling them who his father was and why he was in town, and the guilt was digging its way into his gut and his heart.

What if Caley hated him once he found out, though? What if he couldn't look at Darren again, if he decided they couldn't be together because Darren's father was the head of the dhampirs, the man who gave them orders? That was what terrified Darren the most.

He'd never had anything like this. He'd had lovers, although he wouldn't even call them that. They'd been quick fucks, people he'd never thought about a second time once he was done with them. He knew he would never be able to forget Caley, though. He didn't *want* to forget him, which was terrifying.

"What's going on?" Caley asked, his voice soft and gentle.

He wouldn't push, not if Darren told him he didn't want to talk. It was tempting to do just that, and maybe Darren should. The cafeteria wasn't the best place to tell his boyfriend that his father was the leader of the vampire hunters.

Darren swallowed. "We should probably talk."

Caley arched a brow and leaned back in his chair. "That doesn't sound good. Usually, it's what people say when they want to break up."

Darren shook his head. "I don't want to break up, but it has to do with the thing I haven't told you and Oren."

Caley stared at Darren for a moment before nodding. "I see. You know you don't have to tell me, right? Everyone has secrets, and you're no different."

"Not everyone has secrets that could potentially kill someone."

"That much is true. Still, you don't have to tell me anything if you're not ready."

"I don't think I'll ever be ready to tell you this. I have to, though. I haven't been feeling right since we got together because of it. You told me so much about your life, and I've been hiding this from you. It doesn't feel right, not if we want to take our relationship to the next level."

Caley blinked. "Next level?"

Darren's cheeks heated, and he looked away as he shrugged. "You know. We haven't been together long, but I like you." The cafeteria wasn't the best place to have this conversation, either, but it felt easier than telling Caley about his father.

"I like you, too," Caley said.

Darren shouldn't have felt relieved, but he did. Then he remembered that Caley might kick his ass to the curb as soon as he found out who Darren's father was. "You might change your mind."

"I don't think so."

"You don't know what I'm hiding."

Caley tapped his fingertips on his bottle. "You're right. I don't, and it could be a horrible secret. It won't change who you are, though. It might change the image I have of you in the past, but you're not that person anymore. I don't think I will stop liking you, even if I have a hard time dealing with it."

Darren wished he could be sure about it, but he couldn't, and the thought of telling Caley about his father made him want to throw up the little bit of sandwich he'd already eaten.

"We can go to my office," Caley murmured.

Darren nodded stiffly. "I think it would be for the best." He wasn't looking forward to going to the morgue, but it felt like the perfect place to tell Caley about his father.

The cafeteria door slammed open, and Oren strode in. He looked around, his gaze stopping on Darren and Caley, and he made a beeline for them. From his expression, Darren could tell he wasn't happy. He was never happy when it came to Darren, but this looked different, and Darren held his breath.

Oren stopped next to their table. Before either of them could say anything, he pointed at Darren. "Why did I just get a video message from the leader of the dhampirs asking for his son back?"

The world twisted, and Darren sucked in a breath.

"The leader of the dhampirs contacted you?" Caley asked. He was doing his best to ignore that Oren was still staring at Darren.

Oren finally turned his attention to Caley. "He did. Well, he didn't address it to me, but rather, to the conclave. They sent it my way. They wanted to know what I knew about the situation."

"And *what* do you know about the situation?"

Oren looked at Darren again. "Nothing. I wasn't aware we'd captured the son of the leader of the dhampirs."

Caley swallowed. That was the secret Darren had been about to tell him, then.

"I was going to tell you," Darren said.

Oren slammed his hand on the table between Darren and Caley. "You were? When? When more vampires were killed because your father wants you back? Are you having fun? Or is that why you're here? Did you think that by staying with us, your father would get angry and kill every vampire in sight until he got you back?"

Caley understood where Oren was coming from and why he was angry, but he wouldn't allow him to do this. He stood up, facing his best friend. "Don't talk to him that way."

Oren looked taken aback, but he didn't back down. "What are you talking about? You heard what I said. He's not just a vampire hunter. He's the son of the head of the dhampirs."

"And he's not his father. He wasn't hiding this because he wanted to do more damage."

"Why was he hiding it, then? Because it's the only thing that makes sense."

Caley jerked when he felt a hand on his wrist and looked down.

Darren was shaking his head. "I don't want the two of you to fight because of me."

"That would be a first," Oren snarked.

Caley had had enough of Oren's attitude, but he would go along with what Darren wanted. "All right." He sat down again, staring at Darren. "I think you should explain."

Darren looked around. Everyone in the cafeteria was staring, even though they were doing their best not to look like it. Caley sighed, already knowing they wouldn't go anywhere before having this talk, not unless he wanted to drag Oren.

"The reason I didn't tell you was that I was afraid. I thought you were going to kill me if I told you who my father was."

Oren snorted. "Damn right I would have killed you. You're the next leader of the hunters."

Darren rolled his eyes. "Sure I am. Can you imagine that? It would be a disaster. Why do you think my father hates me as much as he does?"

"It doesn't look like he hates you, since he's looking for you. He demanded we give you back to him. If we don't, he's going to rain blood and fear on the city."

Darren rubbed his face. Since he seemed to need a moment, Caley caught Oren's hand and pulled him down, gesturing at the chair next to his. Oren looked like he wanted to refuse, but Caley glared at him until he sighed and finally obeyed the silent order.

"My father has always hated me," Darren finally said. "I was never cruel enough for him, never good enough. I did my best to get him to love me and to see that he could be proud of me, and now, I regret it. It wasn't worth it, but I didn't have anyone or anything else back then. It would be like the person you love the most threatening to cast you out if you didn't do what they wanted. If I'd gone against his orders, I would have been lucky if I had the opportunity to run away. More likely, he would have killed me himself."

"Why does he want you back, then?" Oren asked.

"Because it's what a father should do. The hunters don't care about love, but even though we all know I would be awful at leading anyone, it's what they all expect. I never thought I would be alive long enough to take my father's place. People expect me to be by his side, though, and he doesn't want to lose face. He needs the hunters to respect him, and one way to do that is to have a strong hand and use the sense of family and us against the world. What kind of reputation will he have if his own son ran away to be with vampires?"

"He doesn't know you're here voluntarily, though," Caley said.

"I wasn't, in the beginning. He probably knows I was captured with the others."

"We killed those," Oren pointed out.

"And I'm sure he knows about that, too. He's only using me as a reason to create trouble. He doesn't expect you to give me back, even if I'm still alive. He'll use your words to show the other hunters how bad vampires are and as a reason to attack. Not that he needs one. Any hunter would be more than happy to attack vampires. But this way, he's justified, and he can show the hunters how good a person he is."

Caley reached for Darren's hand again. Darren pulled away before Caley could touch it, though, and Caley moved back.

He was hurt. He couldn't deny that, but he knew he had to get over it. Logically, he knew why Darren hadn't told Oren. Oren had been pissed just now, and it would have been worse before he got to know Darren. Caley was different, though. He and Darren were together, and he felt like Darren should have told him.

He understood why he hadn't. He'd explained he'd been afraid to lose Caley, and even though Caley wasn't going anywhere, Darren still had doubts. Besides, the fact that he'd been about to tell him had to count for something. He hadn't been planning on keeping this secret forever.

Things between them were good, but Caley couldn't deny they were strange. Darren was in limbo. He was a vampire hunter who couldn't go back, partly because his heart wasn't in it anymore. He was a prisoner, yet he was given a lot more freedom than any other prisoner. He didn't have a job, and he had to follow Caley around all day, every day. It had helped their relationship, but the rest of Darren's life was still on pause, and he knew Darren had a hard time dealing with that.

Caley didn't know what would happen next. They would have to deal with the dhampirs, and hopefully, all of them would make it out of it alive. Once that was over, though, Darren would have to make decisions. A lot of people didn't like him and his presence in the conclave building. Darren had never seemed to care, but now, Caley wondered. Would Darren want to stay here after he was let go? Or would he want to leave the city and have a fresh start somewhere? What about their relationship?

Those were questions Caley couldn't answer now, and he shouldn't even try.

"Would you ever have told us?" Oren asked.

"I was about to tell Caley."

Oren snorted. "That's convenient."

"It might be convenient, but I *was* going to tell him. We'd decided to talk in his office just now. I didn't have time to explain because you barged in looking ready to kill me."

"I wanted to," Oren said.

"I'm not surprised." Darren hesitated. "What's next? I can go back, if you want. It would give my father one less reason to attack."

Caley cried out. "You can't go back to him. He's going to kill you if he finds out what happened while you were here."

Darren smiled at Caley, but it was sad. "Even if he doesn't find out, he'll probably hurt me anyway. He'll be able to see that I wasn't really a prisoner. I'm in too good a shape. Besides, he's going to want revenge for what happened. I allowed vampires to capture my men and me. I have to pay for that." He looked at Oren again. "I don't want to go back. If I had my way, I would never see him again. I'll go if I have to, though. It will give you time, and my father won't be able to use me to attack. Of course, that doesn't mean he *won't* attack. He's a vampire hunter, after all."

Oren continued to stare at Darren. "What do you think would be the best thing to do in this situation?"

"I'm not sure. To go back could help save vampires, at least for now. It won't be for long, though. I don't think he'll keep me alive for more than a few days. It would give you those days to get ready, though."

"You're ready to sacrifice yourself for that?"

Caley shot to his feet. "No," he said.

"Caley —"

"You're talking about sacrificing yourself, about allowing your father to kill you and giving yourself up to him. What do you think I'm going to do? Sit back and watch you kill yourself?"

Darren shouldn't have been surprised at Caley's reaction, but he was. He'd expected Caley to hate him after what he'd just confessed. He wouldn't go as far as to say Caley would want him killed, not after what they'd shared, but he had thought Caley wouldn't care anymore. Instead, he clearly didn't want Darren to go back to his father.

An idea was forming in his mind. It was probably the stupidest thing he'd ever thought about, but he had to do something. He couldn't just stand back and let his father tear through the city to get him back. "I'm not going to allow him to kill me," he told Caley.

"But you said that's what's going to happen if you go back to him."

"But he won't kill me right away. That will give you a few days to plan things out and get ready."

Caley shook his head. "I don't care about that. Don't you see? I'm terrified for *you*. Those few days mean that your father will have time to torture and kill you."

Darren reached out and took Caley's hand. Caley looked like he wanted to snatch it away, and Darren wouldn't blame him. He'd have done the same thing a few minutes ago. Caley was angry, and he wanted to continue to yell at Darren. They were getting too much attention, though, and Darren was re-lieved when he gently tugged and Caley sat in his chair again.

"Hear me out, okay?" he asked.

Caley stared at him for a moment before nodding curtly. Darren squeezed his hand and looked at Oren. "I want to go undercover."

Oren frowned. "Undercover?"

"My father will know something strange happened, since no matter how hard we try, I won't look like I've been getting tortured since I got here. He probably expects me to be dead, and if I'm not, to be in bad shape. He's going to want to inter-rogate me, and that will give me time to learn his plans and hopefully, to take him and his dhampirs down."

"You want to take the entire organization down?"

"Isn't that what you've been looking for the entire time?"

"It is. How do I know I can trust you, though?"

Darren swallowed. "You don't. You're going to have to de-cide whether or not you trust me. I know that not telling you about my father makes it even harder. I know that you never trusted me entirely, and that this secret is one more reason for you to never do so. I truly want to help, though."

"Why? I know you and Caley are together, but none of this makes sense."

Darren leaned back in his chair. He and Caley had talked about this, but Caley was the only one who knew how much Darren had changed. Falkner probably suspected, but Darren had never been as close to him as he was to Caley. "I've al-ways known my father was wrong," he said. He grimaced when he realized how that sounded. "What I mean is that I never believed that what he was doing was right. My entire life, he taught me that vampires were evil. My mother was a vampire, but he barely spoke about her, and when he did, it was obvious he hated her. He told me how she left me, how she'd *abandoned* me. He used her as an example, as well as every attack from a vampire on a human."

"I'm sorry you had to grow up that way, but I don't understand where you're going with this."

"I'm trying to explain. It was easier to talk to Caley, though."

Oren glared. "Just say what you have to say and stop beating around the bush."

Darren nodded. "What I mean is that I grew up hating vampires because it's what I was taught. Once I was an adult and I started being sent out on missions, I killed vampires without hesitation. I've always hated them and never allowed any of them to change my mind. Then you captured me. I was forced to see that not all vampires were evil. Falkner forgave me for what I did to him even though he didn't have any reason to. He stayed by my side, was my friend through all of this. And of course, there's Caley. I *know* vampires aren't evil, not any more than humans or dhampirs are. I never want to kill a vampire again, and I never will, not unless they attack me. That's why I want to take my father down. He's not going to stop trying to kill every single vampire in the world."

Oren slowly nodded. "What will happen if we do take him down?"

"I can't promise it will magically solve all your problems with dhampirs. There are a lot of us in the world, and we don't all belong to my father's organization. Besides, even if you kill him, you won't be able to kill all the dhampirs who obey his orders. It will throw them into a panic, though. He's the one who gives the orders. He doesn't have a second in command or anything like that. He's too paranoid. That means that if you take him down, the other dhampirs won't know what to do. Some might try to take his place, but for the time being, the vampires in the city will be safe."

Caley squeezed Darren's hand to the point of pain. "How can you offer your life like this?"

Oren got to his feet, surprising both Caley and Darren. "I'm going to let the two of you talk about it. Darren, if you're still convinced about it after the conversation with Caley, I accept your offer. We're going to have to hash the details out, though, so come find me in my office."

"How can you do this?" Caley asked.

Oren looked sad when he turned to him. "I don't want to hurt you. I know how much you care about him, and I hope he'll make it out of the situation in one piece. We have the opportunity to get rid of the dhampirs in town and save a lot of lives, though. I can't turn my back on that, even for you."

Caley sucked in a breath. Both he and Darren watched Oren walk away, and Darren wasn't sure where to start. He truly thought this was their best bet. He wanted to do this, even though he knew it would probably end up with him dead.

He owed it to the vampires. He'd killed many of them, and he would never be able to atone for that. He could help the vampires who were left, though. He could make sure their lives were easier, and more importantly, safer. He could save vampire parents and children like the little girl who had been killed.

Caley got to his feet and pulled Darren out of his chair. Darren stumbled, but Caley was there to catch him, and to Darren's surprise, he cupped Darren's face with both his hands and kissed him harshly.

"Nothing I'll say will change your mind, right?" Caley asked.

Darren shook his head. Caley kissed him again, and Darren surrendered.

He didn't want to lose this. He'd never thought he would have a chance at a new life and a relationship. Caley was everything to him right now, and the thought of losing him was the worst thing Darren could think of.

He was ready to sacrifice himself and everything they could have. He had to. He would never be able to get over what he'd done and over his past if he didn't try to make up for it, but he wasn't sure Caley could understand.

"I have to do it," Darren said as he wrapped his arms around Caley.

"You really don't. We both know what your father will do to you if you go back."

"I know. But I *do* have to do it, Caley. It's a chance for me to redeem myself, and I need it."

"I don't care what you did in the past."

"I do."

That was why Caley was going to accept Darren's decision, even though he didn't want to. He knew Darren disliked his past and what he'd done. Darren saw this mission as a way to atone. If he couldn't do it, he would try to find another way, and Caley would no doubt hate that as much as this one.

He didn't want to lose Darren. When he'd first agreed to keep an eye on him for Oren, he'd never imagined their relationship would become what it was now. It had been a long time since he'd fallen in love, but he had with Darren, and the thought of not having this anymore terrified him. He was ready to do anything to make sure Darren came out of this okay, but he was pretty sure nothing he could do or say would change Darren's mind. That meant he would have to find another way to keep the man he loved safe.

"I love you," he said, because Darren had to know.

"Even though I'm human?" Darren asked.

That wasn't what Caley expected. "Why would you being human change my feelings? I wouldn't want you any other way."

Darren gripped both of Caley's wrists. "You know what I

am. What I did. I find it hard to believe you can get over it."
Darren's voice was rough and low.

"I don't have to get over anything. What you did is in the
past. And while I understand you want to be redeemed, I
wish you didn't. You have nothing to be redeemed for. You're
a good person, even though you don't want to accept that."
Caley sucked in a breath. "I won't try to stop you, though.
You've made your decision, and I'll respect it. Now we have
to plan this perfectly so you'll come back because I need you
to."

Darren nodded. "I will."

Obviously Darren couldn't promise, but Caley knew Darren wanted to make him feel better. Nothing would, though,
except having Darren back and knowing he would never go
to his father again.

Since that wasn't going to happen, Caley straightened and
let Darren go. He looked around, just now realizing they'd
made a spectacle of themselves. He didn't care, though. Everyone in the building already knew they were together.
Watching Caley confess he loved Darren didn't change that.

"We should go to Oren," Caley said. "I'm sure he's waiting
for us."

"He said he would be."

They cleaned the table they'd used and left the cafeteria in
silence. As soon as the door was closed behind them, though,
Darren grabbed Caley's hand. He pulled him down the hallway, looked around, and kissed him. "I love you too, you
know?"

Caley couldn't help but smile. "Do I?"

Darren growled. "I sure hope you do. Because I love you. I
didn't want to tell you in front of everyone, even though you
didn't seem to care about that."

"I'm sorry. I know you don't like people to watch you."

"Only because usually, they watch me wondering if I'm

going to kill them. I don't care if they see you and me together. I want them to know you're taken."

Caley smiled. "I'm pretty sure all of them already do."

"Yeah, well, now, I know they do. And I know that you don't like this plan. I don't, either. If I could choose, I would never go back to my father. This is the only way to solve the problem. With him out of the way, the dhampirs won't be as dangerous as they are now. They will disband and leave the city, and it will give the vampires who live here a chance to be in peace. They deserve it, after everything the dhampirs have put them through."

"It wasn't your fault. I hope you realize that. I know you want to redeem yourself with this mission, but getting killed isn't going to please anyone."

"I'm pretty sure Oren wouldn't mind."

That startled a laugh out of Caley. "It's fake. He might not be crazy about you, but he doesn't want you to die."

"I wouldn't be too sure about that."

"You'll see. He's going to help you plan this, and he's going to make sure you have everything you need to come back."

"He'll do it because he loves you, but it has nothing to do with me."

Caley buried his face against Darren's neck. "I think he quite likes you, actually. He doesn't want to admit it because you are who you are, and he is who he is. It's a front, though. I promise you that."

"Well, I hope you're right. I expect to come back. It's not going to be easy, knowing my father, but having you and Oren at my back helps. I have you to rely on."

"You don't just have us. There's also Falkner and a lot of other people. They might not know you well, because you haven't allowed them into your life, but they won't want you to die."

No matter how much Caley wanted to stay right where

they were, they had plans to make, and important ones at that. If they were going to make sure Darren came back in one piece, it would be vital to know what to expect.

He sighed. "We should go."

"We should, yes." But Darren's arms tightened around Caley. "I don't want to make promises I won't be able to keep, but I have every intention of coming back to you. I never expected anything like this to happen between us, but I'm glad it did. You made the past few weeks in my life happy, Caley. Even if I were to die, it would be worth it."

Caley sucked in a breath. He understood what Darren was saying, but he didn't want to listen to this. "Don't say you're going to die, because you're not."

"I can't make that promise. I'll do everything I can to come back to you, though. I'm not giving up on us easily. I want this to last for as long as it can."

"Then we'd better find Oren and start planning."

They separated and finally headed to Oren's office. Caley was tempted to drag Darren home, tie him to the bed, and make sure he couldn't go anywhere, but he couldn't. Darren wanted to do this, and he needed to. It would save countless lives in the city. Caley suspected that if he asked Oren, Oren would look the other way and wouldn't demand Darren do this. He couldn't do that, though. It was Darren's decision, no matter how much Caley hated it.

Oren looked relieved when they walked into his office. "I thought you were going to run away together," he said.

Darren snorted. "I would never do that."

Oren stared at him for a moment before nodding. "I'm starting to understand that. You're not the kind of person I thought you were, Darren. I'm glad I was wrong about you."

Darren arched a brow. "Does that mean you trust me now?"

"I don't know if I'll ever trust you, but if you're good

enough for my best friend, you're good enough for me, too."

"I'm touched." Darren's tone was sarcastic.

It made Caley smile. No matter how much those two continued insisting they hated each other, it wasn't true. They didn't know each other, but they would eventually. Because Darren was going to come back, and he and Caley would have decades together. It would give Oren all the time he needed to get to know Darren, and eventually, they would become friends.

For that to happen, though, they needed to focus on what was next.

"What can you tell us about your father?" he asked Darren as he sat in front of Oren's desk.

Darren sighed and sat next to him. "Way too much. I never liked him, and I'm not looking forward to doing this."

"But you're going to do it anyway."

Darren stared at Caley and nodded. "I am."

And Caley ought to resign himself to that.

CHAPTER SIX

Darren was in pain, and for once, it was intentional. He knew he would have a hard time convincing his father to take him back, but it would be next to impossible if he wasn't roughed up. That was why he'd asked Oren to do it, and even though he'd expected Oren to be happy about it, the vampire hadn't seemed to be. Darren wondered if it had more to do with the fact that Darren was dating Oren's best friend than that Oren liked him.

Now wasn't the time to think about that, though. He needed to say goodbye to Caley, and he knew neither of them wanted to go through that. Darren didn't know whether or not he would ever see Caley again, and that was one more thing he didn't want to think about.

Caley wasn't happy. Darren only had to see his expression to be sure of that. "You wouldn't look out of place on one of my tables," Caley said, gesturing at his office door.

Darren grimaced, and even doing that hurt. "You know this was necessary."

"Do I?"

"My father is already going to be suspicious. If he sees me without as much as a scratch, he'll know something's up."

"Oren didn't have to be so rough."

Darren reached for Caley. He hadn't been sure his boyfriend would allow him to hug him, and he was relieved when Caley came into his arms without protesting. "He didn't want to do it," he said.

"He doesn't like you." Caley's voice was muffled since he

was pressing his face against Darren's chest.

"He doesn't hate me, though. He didn't want to do it, no matter how much he dislikes me. He wants you to be happy, and he knows that hitting me is not the way to make that happen. We both had to go through it, though, and I hope you won't hold it against him."

Caley sighed. "I won't. I might not like this plan, but I know it's necessary." He tilted his head up so they could look each other in the eyes. "Don't do anything stupid."

Darren grinned. "Isn't that what I'm already doing?"

"You are. I want to get you back in one piece, though. Do whatever you have to do to make sure it happens. Go along with what your father wants. Oren won't be far."

"And he'll help me. I know."

"He will because, like you said, he wants me to be happy. It doesn't matter that he doesn't like you. He knows you're part of his life now."

Darren kissed Caley's forehead. "Don't you do anything stupid, either."

Caley shook his head. "What would I do? I'm headed home as soon as you leave."

Darren was pretty sure that was a lie. He wanted to think Caley would stay away, but he knew Caley. He also knew himself, and he wouldn't have been happy staying away when the man he loved was in danger. "You don't know my father the way I do. He's cruel, and if he gets his hands on you, he's going to kill you."

"I said I wasn't going to do anything stupid."

"All right. I believe you." He really didn't, but he couldn't waste more time. He kissed Caley again, on the lips this time, until they were both out of breath. He wanted to stay right where he was, to forget everything that didn't have to do with Caley, but instead of doing that, he took a step back and let go of his boyfriend. "I'll be back as soon as possible."

Caley stared at him for a moment. "I'll hold you to that."

Darren didn't look back as he left. He couldn't let himself.

Oren was waiting for him in the hallway outside the morgue. He nodded at Caley, then led Darren away. "I sent a message to your father. He knows we're releasing you. He'll be waiting for you."

"Where are you supposed to drop me off?"

"Near a phone booth. He wants you to call as soon as you're there."

Darren frowned. "I thought you'd be there when he picks me up."

"I tried to, but your father doesn't want to see any vampires close by when he gets you. I'm sorry."

Darren shook his head. "It's not your fault. I should have known he would be like this. He doesn't trust anyone, not even me." And that would be a problem. It wasn't something Darren had to think about right now, though, so he focused on why he was doing this.

It didn't help as much as he wished it did. He knew he was taking down his father for the right reasons, but he was still terrified.

When Oren dropped him off, Darren watched the car disappear. He was pretty sure someone was already watching him, so he made sure to stumble toward the booth. His father knew something was up, but doing this was the only way to put him out of business. Darren was going to have to play the game, and he hoped he would be as good as his father.

His hand trembled. He picked up the phone and dialed the number he knew by heart. "It's Darren," he said when someone answered.

"Are you alone?" his father asked.

"I am. They left me here."

"Good. Someone is going to pick you up. I'll be waiting for

you here."

Darren shivered as he hung up. He didn't have to wait long until a truck stopped in front of the booth. He recognized the dhampir in the driver's seat, and he nodded at the man when he climbed into the backseat. There was another dhampir in the passenger seat, but he didn't even look at Darren. The three of them stayed silent as they headed wherever Darren's father was staying now that he was in town. Darren had a tracker on him, but he knew he couldn't keep it there. His father would no doubt look for one, and he couldn't allow him to find it. Moving as little as he could so the two dhampirs in the front wouldn't notice him, he took it out of his pocket and pushed it between the seat and the back. Hopefully, no one would find it.

He wasn't surprised when the dhampirs parked in front of what looked like an abandoned warehouse. This kind of place was where his father always settled down when he came into a city. This time wasn't any different. He liked empty warehouses where all the dhampirs could stay at the same time. That way, he could keep an eye on them.

The two dhampirs who had driven Darren led him through the warehouse. Darren was used to the sights, and he barely looked around enough to find the exits. He stumbled a few times so the dhampirs would think he was weak. He'd made sure to look like he'd been beaten up the entire time he'd been with vampires. He'd drawn the line at allowing Oren or Caley to bite him, though. He was nowhere near ready for that to happen, even though it would have been necessary to really sell the story to his father.

The dhampirs stopped in front of a door. The driver knocked, and when Darren's father called out, he opened the door.

Darren had expected to be led into an office. Instead, the room was entirely empty except for two chairs. The driver pushed him inside, and he stumbled, almost falling on his knees. His father, who had been standing by one of the chairs, turned to look at him. "Darren. I wasn't sure you'd come."

"Why wouldn't I? They finally let me go."

"Did they?"

Darren swallowed. "Of course they did."

His father stared at him, and Darren lowered his eyes. "I suppose we're going to find out. Sit down."

The two dhampirs grabbed Darren by the arms and dragged him toward the chairs. Darren had known something like this would happen, and he wasn't surprised. He allowed them to sit him on the chair and stand behind him as if they expected him to run away.

He looked at his father. "They tortured me. You can see that yourself."

His father smiled. "I see that someone has beaten you, yes, but I have no way to know who did or why. You're going to tell me, though. Eventually."

Darren licked his lips. "You're going to torture your own son?"

His father stared at him for a moment. "You know me. I would torture anyone to get the answers I seek. That includes you. Besides, you were stupid enough to allow vampires to capture you. You have to pay for that."

Darren closed his eyes. He didn't see the first blow coming, but he sure felt it.

Caley had promised not to do anything stupid, but he didn't always keep his promises. He knew that what he did next was ridiculous, but when he'd asked Oren to go with him and his team, Oren had told him to go home instead. How was Caley supposed to do that? Did Oren really think he'd be able to sit on the couch and wait for Darren to come back—or maybe not?

No way, which was why he'd followed Oren and the team. He knew Darren was inside the warehouse he was looking at, and even though he couldn't do anything, it made him feel better. If something happened, he would be able to help. He might be a medical examiner, but that didn't mean he couldn't help in a medical capacity. His patients were usually dead, but not always, and if Darren or anyone else needed something, he was ready to do his job.

So he'd followed Oren and the team, but instead of helping, he'd been captured. Now he was in a small room, locked up and bloody.

He looked around and groaned. If the dhampirs didn't kill him, Oren would.

He'd thought that having been an enforcer would be enough for him to be able to defend himself, but obviously, retirement had messed him up. He'd been captured, and he was terrified, both for himself and Darren. What were the dhampirs going to do to them? They knew Caley was a vampire, and he was very much aware of what they did to vampires. He liked his head attached to his shoulders, but he wasn't sure he would have it there for much longer.

He was going to be killed. No one would know what had happened to him because he hadn't told anyone he was coming. Oren and Darren had both told him to stay away, and they expected him to obey. Hopefully, Oren would manage to grab Darren and save him, but he'd have no idea that Caley was in the same building. If Caley wanted to make it out, he was going to have to save himself. It was kind of terrifying because he hadn't done anything like this for years, but he had a chance at a future with Darren, and he wasn't going to waste it.

The sound of footsteps coming closer made him tense. He scrambled to his feet and pressed his back against the wall, not sure what to expect. The sound of a key in the lock didn't come as a surprise, and the door creaked open. Two dhampirs stood there, peeking in. They didn't look afraid, but Caley knew better than to try to talk to them. They weren't friends. They were killers, and they wouldn't listen to anything Caley had to say.

"Go grab him," one of the dhampirs told the other.

The other looked at Caley again. "I don't think so. *You* were given the order. You grab him."

Caley blinked. He'd thought they would be dangerous, and they probably were. They sounded like children just now, though.

"He's going to bite me."

Caley cleared his throat. "I'm not going to bite anyone, although I doubt you'd believe me even if I promised."

The dhampirs finally stepped into the room. "Shut up," the first one snapped.

Caley raised his hands, already regretting his attempt to talk to them. He wasn't going to get out of here, so he might as well go along with whatever they wanted. "I swear I'm not going to do anything."

"You're a vampire. You're a liar." The one who hadn't wanted to come in raised his hand.

Caley sucked in a breath. The blow to his face wasn't a surprise, but it hurt. It threw him against the wall, and he hit the back of his head. They'd roughed him up when they'd found him, but he'd suspected it wouldn't be the end of it. He wished he'd been wrong.

The dhampirs took pleasure in hitting him again and again, or at least, that was what it felt like. Caley curled himself into a small ball, knowing better than to try to defend himself. It wouldn't work. It never did. He waited for them to be done and tried to protect his face. Once they were satisfied, they both grabbed him and jerked him around as they dragged him out of the room and into the hallway.

Caley tried to see through the blood that was pouring from his forehead, but it wasn't easy. They were taking him along the hallway, no doubt to meet their boss. If that was Darren's father, hopefully, it meant the man wasn't torturing Darren.

They stopped in front of a door. One of the dhampirs knocked, and when someone answered from inside, he opened the door. "We have him," he said.

Caley wasn't sure what was going on, but he was brought inside the room. He stumbled, and the dhampirs jerked him around again. They pushed him, and he scrambled to stay on his feet, but he ended up hitting a chair. He supposed it was better than hitting a wall or the dirty floor.

"Tie him up," a hard voice said.

Before the dhampirs obeyed, Caley tried to clean his face from the blood. He wished he hadn't when he saw what was in front of him.

Darren was sitting in a chair, too. Caley couldn't tell if he was tied up, but his eyes were wide, and he'd recognized Caley. Caley tried to smile, but he was pretty sure it came out as more of a grimace, and exposing his fangs wasn't the smartest idea in this situation.

"What's the meaning of this?" Darren asked.

The man who had spoken earlier turned toward him. "You said you didn't betray us. We're going to make sure you didn't."

"What does the vampire have to do with it?" Darren was trying to use a hard tone, but Caley could see right through it, and he suspected he wasn't the only one.

He swallowed. The man standing there had to be Darren's father. He was testing Darren, and he would use Caley to do that. Did he know what was between Caley and Darren? Caley wanted to believe he didn't. How would he have found out? Caley couldn't be a hundred percent sure, and it made him nervous.

Well, even more nervous than he already was.

"You said you were a prisoner, that you still hate all vampires," Darren's father said. He sounded unbothered, and it made Caley want to hit him. He wished he could.

"I do," Darren confirmed. He kept peeking at Caley, though, betraying himself.

"I think it's a lie. I don't know what they did to you, but it's obvious you don't believe in our mission anymore. Did you allow them to bite you?"

Darren tilted his head to the side. "I would have marks if I'd allowed that to happen. None of them bit me."

"And that's what's strange. If you were tortured the way you said you were, why wouldn't they have bitten you? They no doubt knew that it would be the worst thing to do to you. Yet they didn't do it. I'm also suspicious about your wounds. They look fresh, and you don't have many old ones."

Darren stared at his father. "What do you think happened, then?"

"I think that you allowed yourself to be captured. I think it's strange that you're the only dhampir who wasn't killed. There's something there. I think you were weak. You allowed them to change your mind. You allowed them to warp your mind and to brainwash you. You're not my son anymore, and I don't need you to confirm it. The way you're looking at that vampire is enough."

Caley couldn't look away. He wasn't sure what was next, but it didn't look good for him and Darren.

"So nothing I say will change your mind?" Darren asked.

"You could kill the vampire. That would change my mind," Darren's father said.

Darren nodded curtly. Caley knew he wasn't going to do it, so he wasn't worried about that. He *was* worried about Darren, though.

Darren turned to Caley. "What are you doing here?" he asked, clearly not caring anymore.

So that was what would happen. "I'm sorry. I wanted to help."

Darren shook his head. "You shouldn't have come."

Caley opened his mouth to speak again, but one of the dhampirs still standing behind him hit him. Caley's head jerked back, and he groaned.

"Stop that," Darren snapped.

Caley was pretty sure he saw Darren's father smile. "So I was right," he drawled.

Darren should have known better than to admit it, but he needed to save Caley. He wasn't sure he could, though.

His father was going to kill both of them. That much, he was sure of. His father had known something was strange with his reappearance, and he would have found another way to push Darren to admit it if he hadn't had Caley. The fact that he *did* have Caley was horrifying, and if they both made it out of this alive, Darren was going to make sure Caley knew what he thought about the stunt.

First, they had to survive, though.

"What did they do to you?" Darren's father asked.

Darren licked his lips. "Nothing. I told you they kept me prisoner, and it wasn't a lie."

"What happened, then?"

Darren thought quickly. He didn't want to give away everything because that would be the worst thing he could do. Maybe he could give his father something, though. "He was the only one who tried to help me. I don't know why. The others kept interrogating and torturing me, but this one was nice. He brought me food, and he tended to my wounds."

Darren's father looked from Darren to Caley. "Is that it?

You allowed one vampire to soften your heart?"

"Not soften my heart, no. I needed him to survive, and that's why I became friends with him."

"He's a vampire."

"And you taught me to do everything I could to survive. I thought that included befriending a vampire."

Darren could see his father was thinking. He'd been the one to teach Darren how to survive being a vampire hunter, especially if he ended up being captured. He probably hadn't thought about befriending a vampire, but he couldn't deny the results. Darren was home, and his only vampire friend that his father knew about had been captured.

Darren's father finally nodded, and Darren held his breath. "I see. Well, I can't berate you for doing everything you had to do to survive. You're here now, though, which means you don't need him anymore. You're going to kill him."

Darren had known this was going to happen. He'd hoped his father would change his mind, but he wasn't surprised he hadn't. "We don't have to kill him. You can just let him go."

His father arched a brow. "Why would I want to do that?"

"It's not that I want to, but he did help me."

"He should have known better. He's a vampire, and you're a dhampir. He should have killed you when he had the chance. Since he didn't, you're going to be the one to kill him."

Darren got to his feet. His father stared at him, waiting, but Darren didn't know what to do. Even if he attacked his father, they weren't alone in the room. The two dhampirs standing there would make sure he couldn't do much damage, and then, they would kill both him and Caley. They needed help, but Oren's team were nowhere to be seen.

Darren faced Caley. "This was the stupidest thing you've ever done," he said.

Caley gave him a soft, sad smile. "I know. I don't regret doing it, though."

Darren shook his head. "You should. We're both going to die now."

Darren's father tsked. "It's as I thought. You're weak, just like your mother."

The words jolted Darren. He turned to look at his father, but before he could, something hit him on the face. He stumbled back, catching his foot on the chair Caley was sitting on and falling at Caley's feet. A kick landed on his thigh, pain exploding.

He was used to being beaten up, but he'd hoped he would be able to avoid it this time. Clearly, he'd been wrong.

His father was barely out of breath by the time he was done beating Darren up. He was used to this kind of thing. This was one of the ways he liked torturing vampires, and everyone in the organization knew it.

Darren needed answers, though. He couldn't let the pain stop him because this could be the last chance he had. He rolled to his back so he could look up at his father, but his gaze caught on Caley.

Caley had screamed and yelled while Darren's father beat Darren up. He'd begged Darren's father to stop, but it hadn't worked. It had only shown Darren's father that Caley cared for Darren, which wasn't going to help. Caley looked down at Darren with wide eyes. He was pale and obviously terrified. Darren had to ignore him for a moment, though. This was his occasion to find out the truth before dying, and he wanted to take it.

"What did you do to my mother?" he asked. His mouth tasted of blood, warm and disgusting.

His father smiled wickedly. "I was wondering how long it would take you to realize I was lying to you. I knew you were stupid, but I didn't think it would take this long."

"What did you do to her?"

"I killed her. What did you think I did? She was a vampire.

Once she gave birth to you, she wasn't useful to me anymore."

Darren swallowed. "She never agreed to be with you, did she? You wanted a dhampir son, and the only way to make that happen was to have a child with a vampire." He licked his lips. They tasted of blood, too. "You raped her."

His father shrugged. "Her and countless other vampire females. It's not easy to create a dhampir. Vampires aren't very fertile, including females. It took me a while to find the right one."

Darren briefly closed his eyes. He could imagine what his father had done to his mother, even though he didn't even know what she'd looked like. He never would. His father was the only one who could answer those questions, and he'd already said everything he was going to say.

He was the monster, not the vampires. He'd captured, raped, and killed countless vampires. Once he'd managed to get one of them pregnant, he'd kept her prisoner until Darren was born. Then, he'd killed her, too.

Darren was the fruit of rape and violence. He was his father's son. It didn't mean he was going to go along with what his father wanted, though.

Darren tried to get to his feet, which made his father laugh.

"You should stay where you are. It will give you a good seat to watch me kill your friend."

"You don't have to kill him," Darren said. He knew it wouldn't work, but he had to try.

"Why shouldn't I? If I kill him, it's going to hurt you, which is what I want. You need to pay for what you did before you die, and this is the perfect way to make that happen."

"I'm already in pain. You don't have to hurt him to make it worse."

Darren's father was still smiling. "Maybe not, but this is a different kind of pain. You care about him, and it's going to give me a lot of pleasure to kill him in front of you. Once he's dead, you'll follow him. Your death is going to be a lot slower and more painful, though. He'll be the lucky one."

Darren's father reached for his side, where he kept his knife. He was going to stab Caley. That was his preferred way of killing vampires, and it was too easy to imagine him killing Darren's mother that way. Darren hadn't been able to do anything to save her back then since he'd been a newborn, but he *could* do something for Caley.

He didn't allow himself to think about what he was doing or the consequences. His father cocked his hand back, ready to strike. Darren held his breath and waited for the right moment. When he saw the knife arch toward Caley's heart, he jumped to his feet. His entire body hurt, but he ignored it and threw himself between the knife and Caley. The blade sank into his chest as easily as if he were made of butter. It didn't hurt for the first few moments, and he blinked down at the knife.

Then the pain started. Luckily for him, it didn't last long. The world around him turned black, and Darren allowed his eyes to close.

He knew what he had done and that he would have time to regret it later. Hopefully, his death would give Caley enough time to be saved.

Caley screamed. He'd thought he was about to die. He hadn't expected Darren to put himself between the knife and him. He had, though, and Caley had watched as it sank into his chest and killed him.

He tried to get his hands free, but he couldn't. He was tied to the chair, and the only thing he could do was to glare at Darren's father. If looks could kill, he would have killed the man. Unfortunately, they didn't, and he would have to find another way to make it happen.

Darren's father stared at Darren for a moment. Caley expected him to be sorry, maybe horrified at what he'd done. Instead, he barely even reacted. He turned his attention to Caley. "I suppose it's your turn now."

"You just killed your son. How can you not feel sorry and horrified?" Caley spat out.

"He killed himself. He knew what was going to happen if he put himself between the knife and you, yet he did it anyway. He should have known better."

"You would have killed both of us even if he hadn't done it."

"I would have. This way, though, he's going to have to die twice."

Caley's stomach fluttered. In his anger and fear, he'd almost forgotten that Darren was a dhampir. That meant that if he died violently — which he'd just done — he would turn into a vampire.

And if they were still here when it happened, Darren's father would kill him, definitely this time.

Caley couldn't allow that to happen, but he didn't know what to do. He was tied to the chair and surrounded by enemies. Darren was dead, still pressed against him, and he was petrified every time he looked down. He knew Darren would make it if he was given the time and the opportunity, but in the meantime, seeing him like this made Caley want to cry.

"You're going to regret this," Caley said, trying to waste time.

"I don't think I will."

"He was your son. Your heir."

"He was weak, just like his mother." He looked at the dhampirs behind Caley. "You know what to do. Let me know when he wakes up."

Caley couldn't see their reaction, but he could hear the door slam open. Unfortunately for him, his back was to it, so he had no idea who came in. It was several people from the sound of it, though, and he held his breath.

Darren's father reached for the knife in Darren's chest. Caley couldn't do anything but snap his fangs at him, which, luckily for him, was enough to make the man jump away. By the time he tried to reach for the knife again, Oren had walked around Caley. He grabbed Darren's father's arm and slammed him to the floor.

Caley almost cried out in relief. Oren was here, which meant everything was going to be okay. He and Darren were safe.

The next problem was what Darren would do once he woke up. Caley knew how much Darren hated the thought of turning into a vampire. He would rather die than have that happen, yet he'd sacrificed himself for Caley. He'd known that if his father stabbed Caley, Caley would die, but he wouldn't. Instead of dying, he would turn.

He had to have realized that, right? There was no way he had acted on instinct, or at least, Caley didn't want to think so. He didn't want to see hate and disgust in Darren's gaze when he woke up and to lose him.

"Caley?" Oren asked.

Caley blinked. Darren's father was still on the floor, his face pressed against the rough cement. An enforcer was kneeling on his back, handcuffing him, while Oren was standing in front of Caley, reaching for him. When he saw that Caley was with him again, he gently touched Caley's cheek.

"What happened?"

Caley swallowed. "I was stupid."

"I can see that." Oren's gaze moved to Darren. "I suppose I'm going to have to get used to having him in my life."

Caley tugged on his hands. "Untie me. I need to help him."

Oren's expression held pity, but he didn't point out that there was nothing Caley could do for Darren. Instead, he obeyed, untying him from the chair and helping him get to Darren on the floor. Caley knelt next to him, cupping Darren's face with his hands. "Everything is going to be okay," he promised. He stroked Darren's cheekbones, trying to will him into opening his eyes.

It didn't work that way, though. Before Darren woke up, he was going to have to go through a lot. Turning into a vampire wasn't easy for a dhampir. Caley had seen it happen several times when their dhampir prisoners had been killed, and he knew what Darren was going to have to deal with. It would hurt, and he had no doubt that Darren would regret it by the time it was over.

There was nothing he could do for Darren but be there for him, which was what he would do. And if Darren wanted to die once he woke up, well, Caley would give him what he wanted. He wasn't going to think about that just now, though. He didn't know what Darren would think about waking up as a vampire. Maybe having Caley in his life would be enough for him not to want to die a second time. Caley didn't know what he would do if it wasn't and Darren killed himself, but he would deal with it when and if it happened.

"You were late," he told Oren without looking at him.

"There were a lot more dhampirs than we expected. We also didn't expect you to be here."

"It was my fault. This wouldn't have happened if I hadn't been here."

Oren squeezed Caley's shoulder. "We both know that's not true. Darren's father would have killed him even if you hadn't been here. He would have turned him. Darren knew that when he agreed to do this. Don't despair. He's going to be okay."

Caley shrugged Oren's hand off. "You can't know that. He never wanted to be a vampire. He would rather die than be one."

"Things are different now. Don't lose hope, Caley. You don't know how Darren is going to feel about this. He sacrificed himself to save you, and that has to count for something. He knew what he was doing."

"It doesn't mean he's going to be happy when he wakes up."

"We both know he won't be. Being a vampire is everything he's tried to avoid until now. He's been told how awful it was again and again. It won't be easy for him to get used to the idea, but he's not alone. He has you and Falkner."

Caley turned to look at his best friend. "And you?"

Oren grimaced. "And me if he needs me, yes. You love him, which means I accept him."

"Thank you. We're going to need all the help we can get."

"I know. But thanks to him, we captured dozens of dhampirs, including their leader."

"It's not going to stop them for long. There are others out there."

"I'm aware of that. We don't have to think about it now, though. Hopefully, even if there are more dhampirs in town, this will be enough to show them we're not playing around. For now, I think the city is safe, and so are you." He touched Caley again. "You should allow our healers to see you. You're not in good shape."

"I'm fine." Or rather, he would be fine as soon as Darren woke up.

"You're not planning on staying with him until he wakes up, are you? It's going to take a while."

Caley bared his fangs at Oren. "You just try to stop me."

Oren shook his head and raised his hands in surrender. "I like all my fingers attached to my hands, so I won't. I do want a healer to see you, though. Darren sacrificed himself to save you, and he's not going to be happy if he wakes up and finds you all beat up. If you don't want to do it for me, do it for him."

"As long as they don't try taking me away from Darren, I don't care who sees me and what they do to me."

Oren sighed. "I suppose it's better than nothing. Come on. Let's get you to the infirmary and cleaned up. It's going to be a long few days."

CHAPTER SEVEN

Darren had woken up several times. Every single time, his body had felt like it was on fire. He'd barely been able to think, so he hadn't tried. Instead, he'd focused on the soft hands touching his face and his arms, on the hands he recognized and loved so much. Darren had succeeded — he'd saved Caley, which was all that mattered.

Apart from that, though, he wasn't quite sure what had happened when he opened his eyes again. He blinked, staring at the ceiling and trying to recognize it. He wanted to ask where he was, but he was afraid of the answer.

He remembered what had happened. He remembered how terrified he'd been when his father had cocked the knife to kill Caley. He'd barely thought. He'd needed to save Caley, and he'd acted on that instinct, putting himself between the knife and the man he loved. He hadn't allowed himself to think about what would happen if he did it, but now, he couldn't ignore it anymore.

He'd died.

His father has stabbed him in the chest, and it had taken him only a few moments to stop breathing. In those few minutes, he'd had the time to fully understand what he'd done. As a dhampir, dying violently meant he would turn into a vampire, and there was nothing as violent as being stabbed in the chest by your own father.

He tried to sit up, but a hand pushed him back against the pillows. "Don't try to move. You're going to be in pain for a little while longer," a soft voice said.

Darren rolled his head on the pillow so he could see Caley. "You're here."

Caley looked like he hadn't been sleeping or eating. Still, he smiled. "I wouldn't be anywhere else. How are you feeling?"

Darren grimaced. "Like I was stabbed and died."

Caley chuckled. "I suppose we couldn't expect anything better."

"What happened? Where are we?"

"I'll tell you everything as long as you don't try to sit up. You need to rest."

"Fine. I promise I won't try to move. Now tell me, because the last thing I remember is that my father stabbed me. How did you get free? How are we both here?" Wherever *here* was.

Caley patted Darren's hand. "Oren and his team burst in only seconds after you died. They kicked ass and captured your father."

Darren briefly closed his eyes in relief. "So he's never going to hurt anyone else?"

"He's not, no."

"Where is he?"

"In one of the cells here in the conclave building."

"Where am I?"

Caley smiled. "I wanted to keep you at home, but Oren and the healers refused. They thought it would be better if you woke up here, in the conclave building, where the healers could get to you if you need anything. You're in the infirmary."

Darren tried to nod, but his head hurt. *Everything* hurt, which he hoped was eventually going to stop. "What's going to happen to him?"

"He's going to die. So far, he's still human. Oren wanted to talk to you before anything happened. He and the others have already interrogated all the dhampirs, but your father has refused to talk."

"He won't say anything, even if you threaten to kill him."

"I'm pretty sure Oren threatened to kill him only *once*."

Darren chuckled. His ribs hurt, and he raised a hand to press it against them. "He's going to hate that. It would be fitting, though."

"I wouldn't be surprised if Oren kept him as a vampire. He thinks your father knows a lot about the dhampirs around the world, and he wants to take down as many of them as he can."

"I can probably help with that. Not right now, though. Damn, it hurts."

"It's normal. Even though you're a dhampir, your body had to change for you to become a vampire."

Darren swallowed. It had been easy not to think about it while they were talking about his father, but he couldn't ignore it much longer. He tentatively touched his teeth with the tip of his tongue, not surprised when he encountered longer than normal fangs.

He'd known this would happen when he'd put himself between Caley and the knife. His father wouldn't have stopped, not even if it meant killing him. He hadn't expected to live long enough to wrap his mind around the fact that he was a vampire now. The only reason he had was that Oren had intervened and saved him and Caley.

"I'm so sorry," Caley murmured. He squeezed Darren's hand. "I shouldn't have followed you. You wouldn't be in this situation if I hadn't, and I don't know how to apologize to you."

Darren twisted his hand so he could link his fingers with Caley's. "My father would have killed me, regardless. Your presence there didn't change anything."

"I'll understand if you don't want to live this way. I'll help you with whatever you need."

Darren knew what Caley was offering, and it made him

wince. He understood why Caley would think that, though. He'd never made it a secret that he didn't want to be a vampire and that he would rather die than be one.

Things had changed. He'd met Caley, and he'd surprised even himself when he hadn't thought twice about protecting Caley by sacrificing his own life. He knew he would turn if he was stabbed instead of Caley, but he hadn't cared, and he still didn't.

He would do it again if he had to.

He was a vampire. He'd been taught all his life that he should hate himself for having turned. He'd been taught he would be a monster now since he would have to drink human blood to survive.

The thought made his stomach churn. "What does blood taste like?"

Caley frowned but answered. "Not like it tasted when you were human. I know you're hesitant, but I don't want you to die a second time. I don't want to lose you. I can't demand anything from you, especially after what I did, but please. Try drinking some blood and see what happens. It will help you heal."

"I don't know if I can. Just the thought makes me want to throw up."

"I know. You have to try, though. I promise you it's not as disgusting as you imagine. You're not human anymore. There's no going back, only going forward. You can choose how you want to go forward, but I hope it's going to be with me."

Darren wanted to refuse, but Caley was right. He had a choice between dying for good this time or spending the rest of his now endless life with Caley. He was immortal, and while he didn't have to make the decision now, he did have to taste blood. He wanted time with Caley. He wanted to feel good, to be healthy.

He'd already made his decision, hadn't he? Even if blood was disgusting, he would drink it down and like it because it gave him the chance to be with Caley. "Fine. Give me some blood."

He was relieved when Caley took out a stainless-steel bottle from a small fridge in the corner. He hesitated, and Darren wondered what was happening until Caley asked, "I can heat it if you want."

Darren had to swallow. "No. I want it cold."

"It tastes better warm."

"I don't care, Caley. I just want to get this over with."

Caley nodded and opened the bottle. He stuck a straw into it, since he didn't want Darren to sit up, and angled it toward Darren's mouth.

Darren wrapped his lips around the straw. He hesitated, terrified, but he knew he had to do this.

He sucked.

Liquid hit his tongue, and he winced, but it was for nothing. If he hadn't known this was blood, he wouldn't have believed it. It didn't taste coppery or anything like that. Instead, it was sweet and delicious.

He sucked and sucked until, to his surprise, the bottle was empty. Caley was beaming at him, and as he put the bottle away, he asked, "Not that bad, was it?"

Darren shook his head. "Nowhere as bad as I thought it would be. I'm surprised."

"Pleasantly so?"

"Yes." Darren caught Caley's hand and pulled him closer. "I don't want to die again. What happened, happened, and there's no way out of it for me anymore. I'm not sorry, though. I'm happy I saved you, and I would do it again if I had to. I don't regret it. Now that I'm a vampire, we have all the time in the world to be together. That's all I wanted."

"I just don't want you to regret it."

"I can't promise you I never will, but I do know that having you in my life will make it easier. I want this, Caley. I want *you*." Even though he came with unexpected and unwelcomed fangs, Darren wouldn't have it any other way.

You may also enjoy the following from eXtasy Books Inc:

Aaron
Catherine Lievens

Excerpt

Aaron didn't try to be quiet, even though he knew that at least Matthew would already be sleeping. Well, he hoped so. Sometimes, his brother stayed up until midnight, no matter how hard their fathers tried to put him to bed.

Life had been so much easier when Aaron had been an only child.

He never told anyone about this, though. People would tell him he was acting like a child, and they would be right. He was nineteen. He was supposed to be an adult, not to need his parents anymore. It was normal for them to dedicate their time to his siblings. They were young, while Aaron could stand up on his own.

That didn't make him less jealous, though.

He loved his fathers, and he'd had their undivided attention for fifteen years. He'd needed it, and he still did, but now, he felt like they didn't care much anymore. When he forced himself to think about it, he knew he was an idiot, but he couldn't help how he felt. His dads never had time for him anymore, even when he asked. They also barely had the energy. He still needed them, but they didn't seem to remember he was their son.

The apartment was quiet when he got there. He held his breath as he closed the front door, listening, but no one was crying, singing, or screaming. It was strangely calm, as if something was about to happen, and he prayed it didn't.

He knew he was going to be in trouble. His dads didn't want him to jump out the window, although that mostly was because he'd broken a leg once a few years ago. He was better at it now, even though he still shifted as little as possible.

When he stepped into the living room, he found both his dads on the couch. Aaron took a moment to look at them.

They were both tired. That much was obvious. Troy was stretched out on the couch with his head on Emery's lap while Emery carded his fingers into Troy's hair. It glinted red in the light, and Aaron thought about his own red hair.

He looked like both his fathers, which was a strange mix, to say the least.

Emery looked up and smiled. "Then you are," he said.

Troy twisted into a sitting position. "We were getting worried," he said. "I know you're nineteen, but you're still our son. That's never going to change, and neither is the fact that we worry if we don't know where you are."

Aaron was divided between wanting to tell them that he was an adult and that he didn't have to tell them what was going on in his life and being pleased that they obviously cared about him. It meant a lot. "I was downstairs with everyone else. I didn't go out."

Emery nodded. "Good. You said you wanted to talk to us about something. What is it?"

Aaron swallowed. He knew he had to talk to his fathers about what was next for him. He was nineteen, which meant he'd finished high school. He had to make decisions about his future, and he didn't know where to start. He didn't know what he wanted to be, if he wanted to go to college or find a job, or anything else.

He opened his mouth to tell them, but just then, Matthew started calling out. Aaron snapped his mouth shut and glared.

Troy sighed and got to his feet. "I'll get it. I'm sure he only wants a glass of water or something like that."

Aaron knew he had to go, but he still resented it, even though he didn't say anything. His dad already had a hard enough time. He didn't need Aaron to make it even harder.

Still, it showed him that he didn't matter as much. He knew that his fathers had to focus on his siblings because they were younger, but they barely had time for him. They loved him, and Aaron was never going to doubt that, but he needed more than love. He needed their attention. He needed them to show they cared.

"You can tell me if you want," Emery said.

Aaron flopped onto the couch. He didn't want to talk about it anymore, but he supposed he needed to ask questions if he wanted to do what he had in mind. He might not have the faintest idea of what he wanted to do as an adult, but his father had been a vampire hunter. It was in their blood, and Aaron had been playing with the idea that he could follow in his father's steps. "Tell me about your life before you met Dad."

Emery's eyebrows rose on his forehead, but he didn't ask why Aaron wanted to know. "It was hard. I didn't have a home like I do now. I barely had a family. I didn't have time for anything that wasn't hunting vampires. You're already know that, though."

"Was it that bad? I know you lost your family to vampires, but you found a new one."

"And I'll always be grateful. I still miss my parents, though, and my siblings. I miss my aunts and uncles, my cousins. All of them are dead because of vampires and because we didn't stop hunting them."

"You're a Krsnik. It's your duty to hunt vampires. It's what you were born for. What I was born for."

Aaron had said too much. His father straightened,

frowning. "What are you talking about?"

"Nothing."

"Don't lie to me, Aaron."

"I'm not lying. I was just wondering what I could do now that I'm out of high school."

"And you thought you could hunt vampires?"

"I don't know what I want to do, but I'm your son, which means that hunting vampires is in my blood. Why shouldn't I do it?"

Of course, that was the moment Troy walked back into the living room. He heard Aaron's words, and he went so pale that Aaron briefly wondered if he was going to faint. "You're not going to be a vampire hunter," Troy snapped.

Aaron glared. He'd never said he wanted to be one, but he'd been curious. Now that his fathers were forbidding him to hunt vampires, he wanted to do it more than ever. "You can't tell me what to do," he pointed out. "I'm nineteen. I'm an adult."

"Barely, and you still live under our roof. You're still our son."

"I'll always be your son. Are you going to forbid me to do things even when I'm thirty? When I'm fifty?"

Troy's expression twisted, but Aaron didn't know what it meant. "I'm going to forbid you things until you're a hundred if they're stupid and dangerous."

Aaron shook his head. "You won't even listen to me."

"I don't need to listen to you to know what I heard. You're not going to be a vampire hunter, Aaron, not on my watch."

"You can't tell me what to do. And if living with you is a problem I'm sure I can find an apartment in town or even in another town." He turned toward the front door. He couldn't stay here, not like this.

"Where are you going?" Emery asked.

"Away since you don't seem to want me to live with you anymore."

"That's not what I said," Troy tried.

Aaron was angry, though. Just like always, his fathers hadn't listened. They'd jumped to conclusions, they'd forbidden him to do things, but they hadn't listened. Aaron wasn't surprised, but he was resentful. Was it too much to ask for his fathers to consider him a son and to act like they cared about him and his life?

He slammed the front door behind himself, but he didn't stop, not even when his fathers called for him. He knew they would try to find him, which meant he had to leave as soon as possible. He couldn't stay in the house.

There was only one place he could go, and thankfully, it would take him a while to get there, which meant he would have time to think.

ABOUT THE AUTHOR

Catherine is the creator of several series, most of them paranormal, including the Whitedell Pride Series and the Gillham Pack Series. While she graduated in translation, she decided to go the writer's way because it was more fun to create her own stories and characters.

She's been living in Italy for more than twenty years, but she's a daughter of the North—Belgium to be precise—and she misses it so much that she's already planning to move back.

She loves pizza—probably too much—her son, her pets, and of course, books. She sneaks some reading time into her schedule every time she has five minutes free from writing, demands from her various pets and son, and lastly, housework.

Connect with her:

lievens.catherine@gmail.com
BookBub: https://www.bookbub.com/authors/catherine-lievens
Website: https://authorcatherinelievens.com/
Facebook: https://www.facebook.com/catherine.lievens.9
Facebook Group: https://www.facebook.com/groups/411788002341528/
Twitter: https://twitter.com/authorCLievens
Newsletter: http://eepurl.com/c-uvKn